In a Hustler I Trust

Lock Down Publications and Ca$h
Presents
In a Hustler I Trust
A Novel by *Monet Dragun*

Lock Down Publications
P.O. Box 944
Stockbridge, Ga 30281

Visit our website @
www.lockdownpublications.com

Copyright 2022 by Monet Dragun
In a Hustler I Trust

Lock Down Publications
Like our page on Facebook: Lock Down Publications
@
www.facebook.com/lockdownpublications.ldp

Book interior design by: **Shawn Walker**
Edited by**: Kiera Northington**

Stay Connected with Us!

Text **LOCKDOWN** to 22828 to stay up-to-date with new releases, sneak peaks, contests and more…
Thank you.

Submission Guideline.

Submit the first three chapters of your completed manuscript to ldpsubmissions@gmail.com, subject line: Your book's title. The manuscript must be in a .doc file and sent as an attachment. Document should be in Times New Roman, double spaced and in size 12 font. Also, provide your synopsis and full contact information. If sending multiple submissions, they must each be in a separate email.

Have a story but no way to send it electronically? You can still submit to LDP/Ca$h Presents. Send in the first three chapters, written or typed, of your completed manuscript to:

LDP: Submissions Dept
P.O. Box 944
Stockbridge, Ga 30281

DO NOT send original manuscript. Must be a duplicate.

Provide your synopsis and a cover letter containing your full contact information.

Thanks for considering LDP and Ca$h Presents.

A Star is Born

I came in the world as Duchess Brie Lewis, born into a life of drugs, Section-8, gang life, and abuse. But I made it out as *Aquafina*, a twenty-two, going on twenty-three-year-old woman who works at Diamond City in Atlanta, Georgia. I could've gone a different way in life, went to college, worked an honest job, or been a mom of two kids living off child support. But instead, I chose the fast life, it was the only thing I knew. Being cast out by my own family, I had nowhere else to go. This was the only rout I had to find a way to make fast cash.

Strip or something more drastic. Like slanging drugs and I didn't want to go that far.

This was my fast cash, my *"money maker"* that bloomed ever so gracefully. My golden ticket was my bodacious *body*... Hell, I was smart, graduated at the top of my high school class, but the money was something I didn't have growing up in the projects. So, without a full ride, money for school wasn't going to work out. Now that I'm running stacks, I can do anything I want. The person who saved me with a quickness was my brother Tyreese, AKA Reese. He was the man that was there for me through all the shit in my life. He was there for me when no one else was.

People in my life thought I was a hoe, just out here sucking and fucking. I'm not just a stripper shaking my ass on stage, dancing on men, and twerking for hundred-dollar bills. I've never slept with random men for money, and I never will. I was just a young woman trying to make it in this cold world. Hell, my momma didn't show me no better way. I had to make it in the real, big world.

My momma was a hustler herself, never taught me anything I needed to know. That woman is who showed me the bullshit of life. She was always pushing drugs or under her "*man.*" Tyreese taught me everything he could teach me, tried to give me everything Ma didn't. Even taught me about boys... and that was the hard part.

Tyreese truly dreaded telling me the common "birds and bees" story. He wanted to tell me in the worst way, to make me not want to do it ever! Until I was married or at least seventy.

Reese was an overprotective brother, and he had the right to be. What brother wasn't, over their baby sister? He was the one that gave me my *street* smarts, something I would really need in this city.

Back then, I didn't go to parties unless Reese approved. I didn't date unless he thought the guy was worthy of me. I couldn't wear tight clothes, even if they weren't made to be tight.

But shit, of course they were tight. I was thick all over, but it still didn't slide with him. Just because of that, he would put me in a big ass house coat, a muu-muu, anything to cover me if he could. He just couldn't shelter me for too long. On top of that, Reese didn't let me wear obscene make-up I didn't need. And that was only because he didn't want me to turn out like our mother.

And the weave, hell nah. He wasn't having me out walking around with this outrageous, fake ass Remy hair down my back. It's not like I needed it anyway, with our Indian heritage giving me long black hair.

You're probably thinking, why is Reese pretty much my father figure? Shit, it's because my father split when I was born. My brother and I had two different fathers, and his dad had died when I turned seven. The streets are what led him to his death. Then of course, Mom moved on easily and got with some street nigga. That man wasn't, and still ain't shit. He just wanted to cast me out, and he did just that.

He even tried to use my innocent body for his pleasures, but Reese wasn't having that. As much as Reese tried to protect me, it was just so much he could do. And our mother's boyfriend had touched me. I never told Reese this ever happened, because I didn't know what he would do… better yet, I knew what he'd do. And I couldn't see Reese behind bars. He's the only one that's been there for me. We have other siblings, but they didn't like me because of my beauty.

Pretty dumb reason to hate, right? When I told Reese I was a stripper, he was also the only one that didn't cast me out because of it. He loved me and would die for me. Just as I would do the same.

Tyreese was my other half... and a player who knew how the game went. No, he didn't sell or was a dope boy like every other dude in our city. But he knew the tricks and how to spend them. He took his ass to school to be better.

I wanted to do for him for what I couldn't do for myself, I sent him to school on the money I bussed my ass on. I wanted better for myself, but the fast nightlife always drew me back in. Sometimes, I could feel myself wanted to go down that dark path of this lifestyle. I always questioned myself as to whether I'd stop stripping and move onto something better. Will a real man ever love me for me? Or will my fantasy come true and my knight in shining armor come and save me?

Everything around me was tuned out before I heard Miss Coffee shrieking in my ear, "Aquafina! Are you going to get your ass on that stage or what? I didn't hire you to sit here and be scared. Now, get your ass out there on that stage or don't come back at all. Miss Coffee don't got time for the fuck shit." My head turned around at a screaming Miss Coffee who had a serious look on his face.

"I-I'm just a little bit nervous okay, just give me a minute."

"No, hell no. I gave you a minute that turned into ten! Now my customers is waiting for you to come out on stage. I don't need shit getting rowdy in this muthafucka. I am no one's mutha, and I don't got time to baby you. You a grown woman, right? Get the fuck out there," Miss Coffee yelled. This was only my first week here and every time I hit the stage, my stomach was in my chest, and right now I was shitting bricks. It never hit me this damn hard before, and why I couldn't shake it was beyond me.

"Miss Coffee, I heard you, and I'm coming," I said while looking back in the mirror.

"Well, get ya' ass up and make yo' way to that damn stage and shake some ass! Time is money! And bitch, you here to make money," Miss Coffee barked as I stood up. Then I heard *her* voice in the back of my head. It was my mom, talking her shit like she'd always do when drunk. I continued to stare at myself in the mirror as I watched her drunk ass appear before me.

"Look at yo' hoe ass… you ain't gone be shit in life. Look at you, look just like yo' damn daddy. I hate you, you're the reason why he's dead bitch. Can't wait for you to just drop off this earth. Ain't no one gone know who you is no way. Don't nobody know who you are bitch! Duchess, I know you hear me, bitch! Huh!" Her cold words echoed in my head, and all I could do was snarl.

"I am somebody," I murmured while turning on my heels as they echoed loudly on my way to the stage. No matter what, I was going to prove myself to everyone. No one was going to stop me from making it in life. Not my mom, not her asshole of a husband, and damn sure not these pathetic ass hoes in this club. Miss Coffee was right, I had to make this money, this business had no place for weak, or weak-minded bitches. The music blared in the club while I strutted to the stage, DJ Shiesty announced my name one last time and I stepped on stage as the DJ looked at me. "You ready to take the stage with yo' fine ass? They been waiting on you," he said with a smirk on his face.

"So, you kept them dogs down for me huh," I laughed.

"Yeah, you know I got you. You got it, them muthafuckas think you're a star. But guess what?" DJ Shiesty asked as he smirked at me once again.

"What's that?" I questioned him back.

"You are a star, you the baddest bitch here, no disrespect. You the shit, shorty, now go make that ass clap for them dollas." Flipping my hair, I winked at him and nodded for him to play my shit. City Girl's blared through the speakers as I flipped the crystal beads back and strutted to the pole. When I stepped out on stage the crowd roared, and soon the money rained down on me.

All eyes were on me, like I was the baddest bitch in the land. "Y'all niggas ready for me to clear y'all pockets!" The niggas hollered as I grabbed the pole and worked it like it was my last time on the stage. At this moment I was somebody, and nothing could stop me right now. Nothing.

Monet Dragun

Chapter 1

Duchess

"Duchess! Duchess, wake yo' ass up. Now!" My sleep was disturbed by my momma screaming at me out of my sleep. And I definitely didn't feel like being disturbed by anyone in the house. I was extremely tired, and I didn't feel like getting up just to clean the house. The late hours at the club were killing me and now I'm exhausted. A couple nights ago, I was the best bitch in that club, everything I wanted was in my hands, and now look at me. Being told what to do by a woman who never did a damn thing for me.

"A'ight, Mama! Damn!" I said, getting out of bed. I'm the only one who cleans up the damn house. She doesn't make my brother or her husband's sons and daughters clean up anything.

"Make sure you clean the bathroom too." I rolled my eyes as hard as I could before putting on my sweats and walking into the bathroom.

"Get out!" I looked at my stepdad like he was crazy.

"Um, Charles, my mama told me to clean up this funky bathroom. What, you want to do it?" I said with an attitude.

"Girl, don't get yo' ass slapped!" he yelled at me. I brushed past him and left the bathroom. I could feel his creepy eyes on me. "Girl don't get yo' ass hurt," he warned again.

"You ain't gone slap shit, Charles. Last time I checked... you ain't my damn daddy! My daddy dead." He snatched me by my arm, and I pulled back. "I heard you a hoe, stripper, whateva'. Same thing. My son seen you at that club a couple nights ago. I should kick you out my damn house!" he said, looking me up and down like a piece of meat.

"Man, you don't pay any fucking bills! I help my mom with the bills! None of yo' bootleg ass kids don't help none roun'hea! All you do is eat up the food, drink beer, and sit on yo' fat ass! They're nothin' but freeloaders, just like you! Now, lemme go!" My mom was standing there and heard everything.

"So, you gone let ha' lil frail ass talk to me like that?" he questioned my mom with rage. She looked at him, then me. "You need to learn how to control her! It's me or her... and I ain't gone tell you that shit no more!"

"Hold on... Duchess, you're a stripper?" I looked down at my feet. This is not the way I wanted to tell my momma.

"Ma, it's not even like that or what you think—" She cut me off by slapping me in the face. She was taking up for her man, over her blood daughter. Like this wasn't the first time.

"Ain't no daughter of mine gone be a hoe! You wanna be in them streets, then go! You get out of my house! Now! I never should've birthed you!" I looked at her with tears.

"But Mom! You treat me like I'm a dog! How am I your daughter and you treat me like shit? I help you roun' the house, me and Tyreese! His kids don't do shit but sit on they asses and eat us all out of house and home! I just wanted to help you, Mama!"

"Duchess, I'm not about to tell you again. Don't 'but Mom,' my ass! Get out, now! I don't want you here anymore! Gone! Get!" she said harshly as tears ran down my cheeks. I knew this day would come, just not so soon. I turned away from her and ran to my room, getting all my clothes. Her dirty husband came in and snatched the bag away, dumped all my clothes out, and looked at me with a smirk. "You ain't pay for this shit!" he yelled.

I was beyond fed up with him and his bullshit. Snatching my bag back, I slammed the clothes back in it and violently zipped the bag. I've been cleaning this house, not him. I've been paying these bills, not him.

"Actually, I did! You didn't pay for none of this! Yo' ass can't even afford to shave your face or wash ya' own ass! Let alone, pay for the designer clothes I just put back in this bag." I just shook my head, crying. I picked up my purse and phone and grabbed my car keys. "Don't touch my shit. I'll be back for the rest! Yeah, I paid for this too." Flipping him off, I walked out of what used to be my room. I was about to leave when Reese stopped me.

"Duchess, I'm not about to let you be alone out'chea! I just came in to all this yelling. I'm coming with you. We both legal and out of school, I been looking for a place, so I'm coming too." I just nodded, crying.

"Where you going?" our mom screamed towards my brother. "You ain't going nowhere."

"What? With my damn sister! I'm the only one that loves her! We don't need y'all!" He chucked up the deuces and we both left.

"So, where we are going, lil sis?" I looked at him as I wiped my face.

"I have no clue, bro… But the place you mentioned, can we move in today? I'll be damned if we on the streets." Starting the car and thinking about leaving our miserable lives. We just gone start over.

"I don't think that's possible for today. But for sure, this week. We can stay with my girl 'til we lock in on that place."

"Ion want to live under no one else's roof but my own. We can stay there for a few days, even though I have enough money for us to get an apartment somewhere," I said as I sighed.

"Well, I'm in. I'm not about to let you do this alone, okay?" I nodded and we drove to his girlfriend's house for the night. I just can't believe my own mother would do that to me. But figures, since she was an "ain't shit" momma.

Chapter 2

Duchess

Two weeks later

"Aye sis, bring yo' ass here, man!" Reese yelled. I sighed out loud and got up from my very comfortable bed. I didn't want to move, but he was going to keep calling me. So, I flung the cover and sheets off of my body and stood up.

"What on this earth can you want now? What do you want, Reese?" I said to him, coming down the hall.

"Yo' future husband playing..." I looked at the television and the Cleveland vs. Golden State basketball game was on.

"Shut up..." I looked at the screen and bit my lip, watching my crush run across the court. That basketball player was a fine ass man. The dream of being a basketball player's girl-friend, that could never be me. To be blessed with lavish gifts and love.

"See! I knew you liked him, with his big ass nose and hair!" he said, erupting in laughter.

"I hate'chu..." I said, laughing and walking back down the hallway.

"You luh me though!" he yelled from down the hall. I shook my head and continued to walk down the hallway until I reached my room. I could hear him screaming at the TV. Rolling my eyes, I shook my head as I hopped back in my bed. I need to get some rest because I have to work later tonight. I went back into my room and made sure I set my alarm to let me sleep for a good little bit.

The moment my head hit the pillow, I was knocked out and it was amazing. It was as if the light switch went out. To finally get the rest I deserved, without hearing screaming kids, a loudmouth mother, and a nasty man walking around in his drawers trying to creep into my room.

Beep! Beep! Beep!

"Damn, man!" I turned over and looked at the clock before my eyes widened. Damn, I been sleep for five hours. It was damn near dark outside when I looked at the window. No lie, that was the best sleep, ever. Even though I slept well, I had to get up for work and work that pole. I groaned before getting up, walking to the bathroom to get ready to leave.

I turned on the light and looked in the mirror. My hair was a hot mess, there was no way I was about to deal with the thick mane on my head. I struggled to comb through it. I threw some cornrow braids in it, so I could install my thirty-six-inch bundles. I had to have my hair slayed while on that pole tonight.

After doing that, I wrapped my freshly installed weave and put on my shower cap, got in the shower and turned on the nice warm water. I could take a shower as long as I wanted with no one telling me to get out. I washed up with my brand-new yoni soap and rinsed off.

Cutting the steamy shower off and getting out, I wrapped my towel around me and took my cap off. I rinsed my mouth out with my mint mouthwash and swished it around, making sure it made my breath smell good. I needed to be on point to entertain these customers at this exotic gentlemen's club.

Then, I spat out the mouthwash and rinsed out the sink. I went into my room and took off my towel, throwing it on my bed. Putting on some Victoria's Secret lotion and the matching perfume, I then put on my panties and bra, then some gray sweats and a simple gray, PINK tee shirt.

I grabbed my PINK duffel bag and left my room. I walked down the hallway to see my brother laying on the couch, fast asleep. I shook my head before walking over to him. I gently kissed his forehead before shaking him.

"Huh? What?" he said, waking up drowsily.

"I'm off to work. I'll be back late tonight," I told him, making him sigh and nod.

"Be careful, alright?" He deeply sighed, making me nod and wave at him. He waved back, made sure I my grab my keys, and soon left the house.

***

Heading over to Diamond City while blasting Summer Walker's "No Love," I sang along to the lyrics while getting my head in a good space. People thought all strip clubs were grimy, nasty, and full of sex. But all we did was see and sell the fantasy. The owner didn't play none of that shit, if you were willing to fuck and suck in the club, you could do it anywhere else. The women knew better than to try Miss Coffee. See, Miss Coffee was a gay man with the love for sexy women who could dance they ass off.

One thing he couldn't stand was hoes who saw dick before dollas. Miss Coffee knew they would get their coins how they saw fit, but not in his club. He couldn't stop them though, so Miss Coffee had one rule. If you were going to fuck for money, he got a cut and you'd better make sure it ain't a fed. Miss Coffee was a master in the game and had everything on lock and couldn't go down for shit.

Summer Walker's lyrics were hitting me as I sang every note, just to keep my head clear. It's a Friday night, so I know it's going to be packed tonight. And I'm not just talking about packed, I mean "people parking a block away" packed. That's what Diamond City was, the damn spot to be and it was always booming.

Soon, I pulled up and parked in my usual parking spot. My car sparkled as my Hellcat was the best looking jawn in this parking lot. She was a pink and purple color shift, with purple lights at the bottom, and custom interior. Checking myself in the mirror and reapplying my pouty pink lip glossy, I popped my lips and was ready to go. Grabbing my duffel out of the back seat, I popped my car door open and slid out of my car. I locked it up and walked towards the building, slinging my duffel over my shoulder.

"Hey, Bubbles..." I said to the bouncer. Bubbles was a seven-foot, musclebound, almond brown man, with a thick black beard, and golden-brown eyes. His tattoos covered his body like they were a second shirt. He was fine as hell, no lie, but niggas knew not to play with this one.

"Hey, Duchess. It's gonna be wild tonight. It ain't even twelve and that bitch already jumping," he said, smiling as he opened the door for me to go in.

"Ain't it always?" As he opened the door for me, I patted him on the shoulder and went to the dressing rooms. I got greeted by some of the girls. But some of them not so much, it was cool though, I wasn't here to make friends.

"Hey, Duchess..." Leiloni said as she showed off her new outfit, "so what you think?" She started twirling down and working her hips.

"Hey, Leiloni! And girl, that outfit is fire, bitch. Don't tell me you made that yourself?" I said, shocked at how good it looked. Plus, I smiled at how she greeted me like a real woman should. Not all the girls here are nice bitches like her.

See, Leiloni was on a boss-level mindset like me. She was a thick slimy bitch with long green bundles, she always rocked her own outfit designs, and stunned everyone with her real green eyes. To make things even more exotic like she was, Leiloni went by Poison Ivy, her mixed looks made the experience she gave even better.

"Yes, you know I'm trying to become a designer and move on from this place. I'm gone keep posting my shit on *Instagram* until I pop off, girl. I posted a pic of this fit and they went crazy! A hoe might go viral!" she screeched.

I slapped her five as we locked pinkies and screamed "Yas!" I placed my duffel bag on the table and unzipped it as she kept the conversation going.

But as soon as I sat down, Candice came in. I seriously can't stand that hoe. She's the hoe of the century in my book, and everyone else's. The moment I heard her heels click closer, that's when Leiloni dialed down her conversation. She and I rolled our eyes at the same time, as she slipped off to avoid her. But me, I didn't give a shit.

"Sup, Big Booty?" Licking her gloss covered lips, "You looking real nice tonight..." Candice said, eyeing me up and down. "You know I'm gonna be watching you like I do every night. Might just throw a few dollas." She started running her hands through my hair, making me move and look at her crazy.

"Like um, can you not? Don't touch me, I'm trying to be civil," I said, flinging my weave over my shoulder.

"Oh damn, my bad, Big Booty. You just think you the shit now since Miss Coffee made you his top bitch. Girl please, I still run this bitch. And I can *touch* or *lick* on anything I like in this joint," Candice said, twirling her tongue ring and sliding her hand down my arm. Moving again, I was becoming even more annoyed.

"Candice, can you not touch me? I'm not playing with you. Fuck is to you? And Big Booty? The fuck? Go talk that shit to them other bitches, cause it don't work on me. Get yo' ol' ass away from me," I said, getting up and looking at her crazily.

"Why? You know I can still have you, if I want you." She reached, trying to touch me *again*. I wasn't stupid, I knew to stay far from her and my drink too. I wasn't having that, not one bit.

"You know what, bitch, I don't know where the fuck yo' hands been. Probably been in another one of these girl's g-strings. You can get back," I told her, obviously irritated.

"You okay, Big Booty? I'll see you later," she said, smacking my ass and trying to leave the locker room. I was tired of her and that was the last straw.

I snatched her by her blue weave and the wig came off her head. She scoffed and I rolled my eyes at her as hard as I could. She didn't do nothing after that.

"At least I'm not a hoe. Like I said, don't touch me again, or it'll be worse for your ass next time!" I shouted, throwing her wig. I know she heard me because she scurried to the other side of the dressing room.

"Girl, don't stunt her. She the one that tries to get all the girls in here," Leiloni said as I went to my station and started where I left off with my make-up.

"Tuh, I couldn't care less. I don't swing that way. I'm not worried about her at all. She's not even on my level. She needs to get that funky ass smell out ha' mouth. Shit smells like rotten ass and everything. That's probably what she be doing, eating ass. Just ew." She broke out in laughter as I chuckled at myself.

"Leiloni, you're up," the lady said, peeking through the curtain.

"Okay, well here I go, girl. I'll holla' at ya' later." She flipped her hair and got up, checking her make-up one more time.

"Coming to the stage next is the bombshell who captures every man, with those sexy eyes and bubble butt!" DJ Shiesty yelled, making Leiloni look back at the pearl beads that swayed from the door.

"Okay bitches, let me get my thong out my ass and go shake it! I'm coming money!" She got up and sashayed out of the door and I just laughed and so did every girl in the room. I went ahead and put on my Supreme top and finished applying my make-up.

I began to coach myself like I do every time before I go on stage. "Duchess, this is all for the money. Don't get caught up in this shit, the money or these hoes." I opened my eyes and looked at myself in the mirror.

"Show time."

Monet Dragun

Chapter 3

Duchess

I took off my outfit, heels, and what little make-up I had on. "Girl, they said all the big ballers were in hea' tonight," Leiloni's twin Drika said. That girl got the most gangsta stripper name in this piece, Draco. But she got that name for a reason, cause she be clapping niggas with that ass she had on her.

"Girl, I know," I said, placing my bag of money on the table. She started laughing before adjusting her clothes. I was just about to rubber band my money as I sat down on the velvet couch, and about to take out my Glock, cause these bitches was slick. But just as I was about to do so, Miss Coffee came sashaying into the dressing room.

"Miss ma'am, get'cho ass ready for the next set while you in her playing making *TikTok's* and shit, Drika. Time is money, you know this," Miss Coffee said as he strutted in with six-inch heels on, a bomb wig, and a silk pink Gucci suit on. Soon as Drika scrambled to fix herself up and headed out the dressing room, Miss Coffee looked my way, his diamond stud earrings and nose piercing gleamed in the light as he popped his gum.

Miss Coffee was a sharp and sexy man, and his drag was always on point. He looked me up and down, he always drooled over my fits, my taste matched his and he knew I had the drip. "And you, miss girl, you got the spotlight. Duchess, someone wants a private dance. Like now, so get dressed in your best shit and make him drool and rain them dollas. He sho look daddy-ish with fat pockets, so work yo magic." I laughed and nodded as approval.

"You know I got you, Miss Coffee. I keep it juicy," I said, sticking my tongue out as "Juicy" by Doja Cat boomed in the club. He fanned me off as he laughed as well and flipped his hair. I got up and grabbed my sheer mesh and satin two-piece top and shorts that dripped in diamonds. And topped it off with my diamond bra and G-string, custom made by myself.

Miss Coffee stopped in his tracks as his heels skipped and clicked, as his mouth dropped. "Now, Miss girl! Uh-uh, I'ma have to get that off you and squeeze my thick ass in that! Ouf, once he sees you, them stacks gone look nice and lovely! Gone na!"

Laughing, I shook my head. "I'll do the damn thing, Miss Coffee, let me hurry up." I applied some lip liner, pink lip gloss that was extra shimmery, and touched up my highlighter. I flipped my hair to the front and grabbed my flat iron and flatted out a few kinks, so it was back to being bone straight. Popping my lips, I clipped on my diamond bra and slipped on my G-string as my ass was bouncing. Then I boosted my boobs, making my cleavage pop before I put on the mesh satin top and shorts. I got up from my table and mirror and was on my way to walking out of the dressing room.

All these females were looking at me sideways and I was getting tired of it. "What's good? Fuck! Keep your eyes over there, damn," I said as authority came to my side. I strutted from the back and to the main floor. I was frankly sick of this lifestyle and the women that went along with it.

Walking to the private rooms section, I took a deep breath. "It's a dog-eat-dog world out here, bitch," I said, coaching myself again. I opened the door and the hottest, most notorious hustler in Georgia was sitting in the red, leather chair.

Versace, aka Yaheem Carter. He didn't give a fuck about people knowing his real name. He sat there in a silk red and black Versace button-up shirt, partially open, showing his muscles and tattoos. With his black slacks, and Versace loafers, his turban topped off his look along with his diamond earrings that was dripping. This man was a special kind of fine, he had that 90s men kind of fine. And not to mention, he favored Omar Epps back when he played in the movie *Love & Basketball*. He stood out because the red illuminated him as he sat in the tufted seat. He had my body boiling and butterflies in my stomach.

For whatever reason and for the first time, I was intimated by a man's presence. It was something about him, I don't know. *But Lord, help me get through this private dance.* He sat in the chair staring me down, with a particular look in his eye, looking sexy as hell with that cute little smirk that showed his gold grills in his mouth.

I had to keep my composure, but he stared at my tattoos and curves as the lights in the room bounced off my shimmering outfit and bit his lip. *God, why do you have to do this to me?* This was the first time I wanted to break down and do some things I knew I'd regret, but this was my job and I had to be professional. And sell the fantasy.

"So, you're my entertainment for tonight, huh?" He chuckled, putting his blunt out as he waved his index finger for me to come his way. I smiled and walked towards him, making sure my hips swayed from left to right. He whistled in awe. "Damn girl, milk did yo' body good! Mph-mmmm."

"Yes, I am, Mr. Carter. And yes, it did with all these curves, that a problem?" I asked as I put both hands on the leather arms, bending down in front of him, face-to-face.

"Nah. Not at all, ma. You sexy as fuck," he spoke, making me giggle as I sat down on his lap.

"Can I put you on cloud nine, daddy, and take you there?" I asked him.

"Do your thing, ma," he said, making me bite my lip and I began to move my hips as "Streets" by Doja Cat began to blast in the room.

I mouthed the words sexily as I got closer to his ear. *"I been going through some things, I struggle with my inner man, I hustle, I'll do what I can to get this money..."* Then the beat boomed and her voice swayed through my body. As I moved just like Doja did in her video, I hit every beat as the bright red dimmed down. Yaheem bit his lip and watched me. Peeling my mesh top off before she got to the best part of the song, I swayed and dipped as I dragged my hand up my leg to my shorts and spun around in my tall heels. Slapping my ass in the process as it jiggled, I bent over as I arched my back and slipped my thumbs into the sides of my mesh shorts, pulling them down slowly as I swayed my thick ass in his face.

"Damn papa, you a rare breed, no comparing And it's motherfuckin' scary.

Tryna keep him 'cause I found him. Let a hoe know I ain't motherfuckin' sharing I could take you to the parents, then to Paris."

I unclasped my bra and let it fall to the floor. I turned around so he could get a good view of my full plump breasts as I trailed my hands up to my breasts and squeezed them. As I continued to sway my hips, all while bring my fingers slowly to my mouth, I sucked on them. As the beat switched up, so did this ass. I began to slowly walk over to Yaheem and turned around as I circled my ass in his lap. I moved it up and down, making it bounce as I felt his print against my ass. Let's just say his friend surely wasn't little.

I laughed and moved his hand. "No touching," I said before going back to doing what I was before.

"Damn," he mumbled when I grabbed his knees and leaned forwards, starting to twerk in his face. He slapped my ass hard, making me laugh. I guess he couldn't care less about the rules.

I sat back down and grinded on him, as I pressed my back against his chest, biting my lip. "Give me some head," he mumbled into my ear, making me stop and turn to him.

"What?" I asked, making him grip my hips and pull me closer to him.

"Suck my dick," he said in my ear, making me look at him like he was crazy.

"I'm not allowed to do that and I'm not a hoe," I said to him.

"I don't give a fuck about rules, baby girl." He smiled at me. "You want ta make some extra cash tonight?" he asked, putting a huge stack on the table. I was making money, but this was just going too far.

"You're done, okay? You're fine and all, but I'm not gonna do that. Maybe you need anotha' chick, cause it sure as hell ain't me," I said with nothing but attitude.

Yaheem began to laugh and now I wanted to know what the fuck was so funny, "Damn girl, you a feisty one, ain't cha? I like that..." He paused, slapping the fuck out of my ass and thigh. "Coo' it, baby girl, it was just a test. I wasn't about to have you do that shit for real," he said with a smirk, making me raise an eyebrow.

"You must've been doing too much of that Molly, hookah, dope or whatever you was just smoking, cause I'm not suckin' any dick, even if you are known roun' these parts."

He chuckled at me before throwing his hands up in surrender. "Well, can I at least finish gettin' my lap dance? I mean, you know what you doing and you doing it well, and I'll still give you that extra stack." He smirked and licked his lips, looking me up and down, pretty much sizing my ass up once again. He held me down on him.

He was about to say something else, but the door opened, and Miss Coffee came in. "Time's up! Cause I said no touch,

Mr. Carter. You know the rules," he called, making me get off Yaheem and picking up my bra and other garments.

Before I could leave out, Yaheem stood and gently grabbed me by my chin and smiled at me. "You're too beautiful to be doing this, yo. I see what you don't see in yourself. If you gone do this job, don't be scared to do nothing." I looked at him and had no words at all. Yaheem had me questioning things I didn't understand.

He smirked and slipped me another huge stack, two to be exact. He gave me four stacks in total, the most money made in one night at Diamond City. I blushed and walked out, leaving him to leave out behind me and join his crew as they went to the back of the club.

I couldn't help but stare as he walked off. He dapped up his people as the bottle girl came around and he snatched up a glass of liquor. Yaheem was a fine dark chocolate man, his tattoos took well on his skin, his waves were popping, and not to mention, he looked about six foot two. And I was caught up staring.

"Aye, mamasita! Get ya' ass in the back. Lookin' all dazed and mesmerized." I rolled my eyes at Messiah, one of the bodyguards, then made my way back to the dressing room. I made five grand in one night, just from the private dance. This was just too much easy money.

Chapter 4

Duchess

Gripping my duffel in one hand and my bag of money in the other hand, I walked out of the dressing room fully clothed. Even though I was sporting sweats and sneakers, men still whistled at me, which wasn't much to me. I'm used to it. After all of this, I still can't believe what he asked me to do! No man has ever come into this place asking me to suck they dick, especially for cash! They knew better than to try me, but Yaheem was bold as hell.

As much as these females bragged about sucking and fucking for cash, and how much they made in one night, I just couldn't do it. I was so much better than that. I got distracted from my thoughts as Kali, another one of the strippers, spoke to me. "Girl, look at him. He is fine! I'd do anything fo' him. I'm gettin' hot just thinkin' bout it," she said, licking her lips. Kali was one of those types, but she didn't brag about it.

I didn't even hear Kali talking to me. I found myself staring at Yaheem as he walked away with his crew. He looked back at me and smirked.

He even mouthed something, but I didn't catch it because Kali was all in my ear. "So, I see he paid you a lot of gwap, girl! Damn, what you do to the man? Did you give him that throat?" she said, laughing because she knew I wasn't with that.

I looked at her and fanned Kali off, she should know I wasn't into that shit. I wasn't a hoe and that wasn't going to start today. "Just danced, that's all," I honestly told her. I could see the green eye in her and hear the venom in her throat as she spoke.

"Mmm-hmm, that ass is just magic, huh. Girl, it's three a.m. Time for me to take my ass home." I shrugged. I could just see her side eye me as I was about to walk off. Candice was flirting with one of the new girls, as usual. She looked at me and blew me a kiss towards my face. I flicked her off and her face dropped.

I rolled my eyes while making my way out, I didn't have time for these bitches. As I walked out the back, I caught Bubbles before he walked back into the building. "Aye, Bubbles, mind walking me to my car? Miss Coffee really need to get these lights fixed out'chea. You know I got the most bank, I just want to feel secure, you feel me?" He nodded.

"You know I got you, Duchess, you have a good night and get home safe, shorty." Dapping him up, I hopped into my Hellcat, started her up and revved before pulling out.

"Thanks, Bubbles, be easy out'chea." Bubbles tapped the hood of my car and stepped back as I drove out. I had to make a stop somewhere and get some food. The only spots still open this late was Waffle House and McDonald's. And honestly, I didn't feel like dealing with waiting for my food, I just needed it fast cause a bitch was starving.

Stopping by McDonald's, I drove into the drive-thru and ordered up a fresh large fry, and Big Mac meal, with a diet Coke. I made sure I thought of my brother, so I got Reese a ten-piece nugget, medium fry, and sweet tea. I paid the people and drove off, making my way home. I knew my brother would be up when I got home. He waits for me every night when I come home late from work, just to make sure I'm okay.

I got out of the car and walked into the house. "Hey, Tyreese," I said, dropping my bag down.

"Hey, Sis. Now can I go to sleep?"

I laughed at him, nodding before giving him his food. I walked into the kitchen and washed my hands. After that, I went into the living room, plopped down on the couch, and turned on *White Chicks*. Laughing and enjoying my relaxation, I ate my food and quickly fell asleep after.

***

Yaheem

"Aye, mane, we going to the Diamond City club again tonight?" Trigga asked me.

"Don't we always, mane? Just make sho' you bring them stacks..." I said, laughing.

"Yaheem, mane, you the one who be tipping em' big. You like dem' BBWs!" I busted out laughing at him.

"Nah, mane, I like the slim thickems." They all busted out laughing. It was getting late, and I was thinking about ol' girl, like for real. I just couldn't get her outta my head, it wasn't just her banging body, but her in general. It was her personality that really caught me.

"Ight mane, but first we gotta make this drop, then we'll go. I got shit riding on this, the shops gotta pay me. The fuck? I'm not a bank, a loan is a loan. And that shit gotta get paid back in full." I said to my crew, which resided of: Trigga, Justus, and Malachiah. We been running these streets since we was teens and that wasn't stop anytime soon.

Justus got off the phone and looked my way, "Yo, that nigga on 15th Street said he want that dope, that imperial shit, that pure cocaine. This crackhead got bank though, he tryna buy up the shop. I'ma head that way, then meet y'all at Diamond City. When you want us to run at the spot and check on the hoes brewing the snow white?" Justus said. Trigga and Malachiah looked from him to me.

I shrugged. "You know this score, hit the block and get that shit to him so he not blowing up my cell, then slide to the joint and see how them boards holding up. Shoot me a text and make sure all adds up, feel me? And make sure they bag that shit up before they try and slide." Justus nodded.

"I got you, Versace. Aye, I'ma head out, that crackhead phoning me. I'ma slide y'all way tonight so I can throw some money on the fat booty hoes! Be easy," Justus said.

"Be easy, yung!" He dipped off as he was setting up some calls. I got a text from my cousin Bubbles, saying *she* would be there tonight. Long as I could see her shaking that ass, I was going to be straight. We all left from the studio, and we got in my Benz truck. We had a few girls with us, but none of them really caught my eye. I was tryna get with ol' girl, these other chicks didn't match her vibe.

We're headed down to the trap first and then to Diamond City after. After handling business, we got there and the place was bumpin'. The ladies were lookin' right, the drinks slapped, and the music was live. Mami's was shakin' right on beat. The clicking of heels were louder than the music and we knew of only one person that could be. "Good to see you *men* are back, my *best* customers. Of course, we have your VIP section ready. Always the best for you, Mr. Carter," Miss Coffee said as he had his bottle girls show us the way.

"Dope shit, Miss Coffee, you know yo' ladies are in good hands." I laughed.

"I'm already knowing. Have a great time, it's about to be some fire shit tonight, yas!" Miss Coffee snapped his fingers as he walked off. I looked around the spot as I scoped out for that girl from the other night. I can never forget ha' face or her body.

"Aye mane, who you lookin' fa?" I looked at Trigga and shook my head.

"No one dawg, damn, just lookin' at all da fine honeys," I said, dapping him up.

"True!" Some girls came over to our section and started dancing up on us, but I wanted Aquafina. Just when I was thinking about her, Miss Coffee got on this mic. "Welcome to the hottest joint in Atlanta! We got all the exotic bitches that can clap ass in several different languages! We got the fantasy and y'all got the coins! So, make it rain, cause we got some shit for y'all tonight, ya'hemme. Yas, so take out them racks and showers my hoes with that dough. Your king has spoken! Now, DJ Shiesty, spin that shit!" Miss Coffee walked off the diamond stage and DJ Shiesty came up to the booth as smoke began to rise.

"Alright, ladies and pimps! The lady y'all been waiting on all night is about to hit the damn stage! Everything on her jiggles like water, and her moves are like a waterfall. She takes all ya' money and pulls all da' honeys! She a slimy with a nice bounce and got all da' juice. Give it up for the baddest jawn in the land... Aquafina!" We had a good ass view.

I stood up and started throwing money as soon as she came out. She started twirling around the pole and making that ass clap. Her moves were like no other and I just had to have her. Flagging over Miss Coffee, I told him I wanted another private dance from her. I licked my lips as she worked that pole, it was just something about her.

Monet Dragun

Chapter 5

Yaheem

I waited for Miss Coffee to send one of the bouncers over to come and get me for my private dance. As I watched the other strippers work the pole, stripping out of their outfits, and money falling like rain. Sipping my Hennessy, I found myself thinking hard as my mind became clouded.

I ain't gone lie and say I haven't done wrong in my life. I've been hustling since I was fifteen, back when I used to run with my brother. Hustla is my middle name and I live, breathe, and *own* this shit... but nowadays at the age of twenty-five, I was searching for something different in my life. Giving up the streets was never going to happen, that shit was in my blood. But the urge for something more had me yearning for a wife, couple of crumb snatchers, and a life without heart-ache.

Me and my crew slid into the club. All eyes were on us as usual. All the hoes were on my woes. That's the norm out'chea in these parts, people know my name. But they bet not speak of my name in the wrong term, unless they'll be six feet under. I don't play about mines or my money.

Bubbles waved me down, I nodded his way as I guzzled down the last of my Henny. "Aye, Trigga, I'm finna be in the Private Room," I said as I grabbed my bottle of Hennessy from the platter that the thick waitress came by with.

"Ight blood, be easy." I nodded as I slipped my freshly rolled blunt into my parted lips. I looked around at the scene in front of me as dudes who couldn't afford the private rooms got small lap dances. The girls on the pole *making they money,* playas in the private sections *dealing.* I know everything that goes on in here and if anything, if the girls needed coke, it ran by me.

"We brought some ladies for you, Mr. Carter." I nodded and motioned for ha' to send em' in. I didn't care about them, but I didn't want to be rude either. Shit, ass was everywhere, and they just wanted to cop a feel. A variety of beautiful women sashayed into my domain. "Hey, big daddy..." one of them purred. But, at this moment I only had eyes for one woman, Aquafina. And I wanted her, not them. I wanted ha' to myself... privately. I just couldn't take my eyes off her. But, I knew all too well she couldn't handle my life.

***

Duchess

I was twirling on the pole and niggas were going crazy. As I finally descended into a full split and popped my cheeks, money flew. Looking into the whooping and hollering crowd, I spotted Yaheem eyeing me so I did some moves. He threw hella bills and not ones either. The girls in his section were jealous that he was paying more attention to me than them. Especially Candice.

After the last song went off, I got off stage, collecting all my money. I'm the new Pole Assassin Freaknik here at Diamond City. I strutted off to the dressing room, only to be stopped by Miss Coffee. "You gotta another request to be in the private show room again. But, in room 13..." Room 13 was the biggest show room, with mirrors everywhere, the most expensive room at Diamond City. Only one big baller here in this city can afford that, touchy-feely Yaheem Carter but better known as Versace, the biggest hustler in the city. This man got his name from blowing niggas' heads off while dripped in Versace. And he had been that way since he was young. Everyone knew him, his story, and who the fuck he was, he made sure of it. And if they didn't, he was going to show them why he was top notch. *And he wanted to see me again!*

I groaned to myself. He was fine, and his presence spoke volumes. The vibe he gave off made me think he wanted me, but I have no time for a relationship... period. I have my priorities. I flipped my hair over both of my shoulders as I walked away, and then I felt someone grab my wrist.

"What the... *Marco*? Don't touch me! What do you want?" I stated with pure venom in my throat.

"You gone stop talking to me like you crazy, I miss you, yo'!" The liquor on his tongue said it all. I put my finger to my nose and rolled my eyes.

"Are you done, Marco? I'm working and I don't have time for this shit. It was a one-time thing, let it go. Bye!" I said, waving him off. His grip got tighter. "Nah, you're done." I snapped my fingers for one of the bodyguards to come and get this fool.

"Oh alright, this how you do me, bitch? Fuck you, bitch!" Marco screamed.

"Uh-uh, get his ass out my club. Can't hold his liquor, get the fuck out!" Miss Coffee yelled. I groaned and went to the back. This was just too much, and I had to get my mindset straight. I changed my outfit and touched up my make-up.

"Someone got a big baller again! She is taking all the money!" Leiloni groaned and pouted like a big baby.

"Girl, y'all twins and hit the pole at the same time! Double the funds!" I said. They both gave me the "bitch please" face. I laughed and got up when I heard Messiah, one of the bodyguard's, whining voice as he called for me to come out because my private room was ready for me. "Gotta get this money."

"Bandz to make ha' danceeee!" the twins shouted out as I stepped out the door, and my heels clicked. I shook my head as Messiah stood back. This room was so expensive I needed to be led back here. Switching my hips and ass to the very, very back room, I coached myself like I always do. Put on the best sexy seductive smile ever and opened the door. He sat there, pants halfway off his ass sagging, Versace turban on, sunglasses, and not to mention his outfit was too trill. Yaheem peeled his Versace Medusa shades off slowly. revealing his eyes, and they were so sexy, I mentally groaned to myself. I flipped my hair as I stood there staring him down, like he was doing me.

He cracked a smile and his gold grill shined from the show lights. "Come on ova' hea, lil mama..." I smirked back and walked towards him, as my body showed from every angle of the mirror walls of the room. The music started to play, and Teyana Taylor's "Maybe" blasted through the speakers.

"I say boy you done did it
Love how you kiss it
Ooh you can get it
I never felt like that before
Ooh, you the realest
Yeah, I admit it
All in my feelings, damn..."

"Yeah, baby girl, come get this work..." Inside I was screaming, why me! But, once again, this was my fucking job. But this wasn't a part of the plan, and the way he was looking at me was something different.

He licked his full thick lips as I whined my hips to the beat and smiled as I walked over to sit in his lap and twirled my hips on his crotch. He groaned in pleasure as his lust-filled eyes look up at me. You know, that look when they look all innocent and cute. Like y'all teenagers and in love, well puppy love? That was the look on Yaheem's face, and the first time any man has looked at me like that.

His hands fell onto my hips as he guided me, and I could feel him moving his hips upward to match my moments, it was just a vibe. The way our bodies were syncing had me feeling like we were having sex... It was different. "Tell me something, what's ya' name since you know mine?" he asked lowly.

"Uh, Duchess..." I said lowly back to him, it was like he had this kind of hold over me.

"And another question, ma," he said even deeper.

"W-what is it?" I don't know why I was like this around him. He is no different from any other man here. Thug or pimp, they're all the same to me. But fuck, it was his aura that just captured me, that and I couldn't put my finger on it about Yaheem.

"Why you do this? I can see in you... That you got more to you than this..." I lost the feeling right then and there.

"That's none of your damn business, okay?" I instantly grew angry and was about to get off of him.

"Hold up! Wait... I ain't mean it like that. Or for you to tell ya' life story, ma, I apologize." Looking him in his eyes, I softly nodded, and I felt him jerk me hard on his dick. I closed my eyes, because it felt so damn big.

"It's just temporary," I said in a whisper, "I got bigger dreams than this... this is just fast money." Yaheem nodded. I knew of all people he would understand me.

"I get it, I really do. You got something to make it out this joint no lie." As Teyana Taylor continued to play throughout the speakers, I switched up the tempo as got on my knees and bounced my ass to the beat.

"Mmm, what you doing to me?" I asked, losing myself in his brown eyes.

"Aw, you feel me, huh?" he exclaimed. I just put my hands on the top of the chair and really started grinding on him. "You know... I rented this room for the whole night, just so I could have you fo' the night. You don't gotta sho' yo ass for no otha man... Except for me," he said with a chuckle.

Damn, how much did he fucking pay?

He stopped me from what I was doing and looked me in my eyes once again as the music blasted. "You know I can take you away from all this, righ'? I can make ya' whole world change in an instant... Hell, with a snap of my fingers, you can be outta here." I stared into his black orbs. It could've been a way out, a way out from all the pain and bullshit. Just like that, just that easy. But I was no gold digger, and I had no feelings for this man. He was just my payroll.

"I'm fine where I'm at," I spoke. He had a look of disappointment.

"You sure? Cause, I can touch you like this all day..." His big dark skin hands roamed my smooth skin. His kisses were so soft, it made me shiver. I let his tongue lick against my neck, and I shivered once more. He must really love him a stripper. "You wouldn't want that, baby? Huh? Talk to me."

His accent was pleasure, his hands were pleasure, and the words he spoke was pleasure. Everything about him was pleasure and on everything, I wanted to cop a feel. His fingers intertwined with my lace thong against my round ass. He sucked on my neck and grinded against my area harder this time, it was getting too hot and heavy. And I was going to cave. "Tell me..." Yaheem said against my lips.

"Tell you what?" I said breathlessly.

"That you want it... Tell me and I'll gladly give you something to really feel." He gripped me tighter against him and I was going to lose it at any moment. And that point came when I felt his hand slip into my thong. This wasn't me! This wasn't me! I went from refusing his dick, to him fingering me. My head dropped back in pleasure and ecstasy. "Oh, my God..." I moaned out lowly.

"Damn, you tight, I know this shit gone feel good. How long has it been?" he asked, and I shrugged. "Mmm, you sure it's been that long? I can tell cause this shit gripping my finger like a glove..." I nodded and I felt my bra being removed and my breasts were set free. His mouth and tongue latched around my right nipple and his finger pumped.

"Oh, shit... Wait, this ain't me, stop, please..." I moaned out, trying to get his finger out of me. But he wouldn't let up.

"What you mean this ain't you? You are not a hoe, baby girl... Just lemme make you feel good just this one time. Come on, come on... Cum for daddy." I grabbed the back of his neck as he pumped faster and curled his fingers inside my wet pussy. Then he put my whole tit in his mouth.

"Shit... Yaheem, why you doing this to me?" I whined as the music covered my much louder moans.

"I can do way more that this... Have you losing your voice." Those words echoed in my brain. The same words my no-good stepdad said to me as he let his son rape me. I forcefully pushed Yaheem out and stood up weakly, nearly falling. "Why you make me stop? You good?" He questioned as he stared up at me. "Duchess."

"I can't do this... This shit is not me!" I could hardly pull up my thong because I was so flustered. I felt Yaheem's arms snake around me. "Whoa! Whoa! Chill, ma, what just happened? You look like someone kilt ya best friend! Did I hurt you?" I shook my head no as I kept myself from breaking down. "Then what is it? I wanna get to know you betta..." His arms wouldn't listen. But I couldn't do this. I pushed him back, but he quickly picked me up.

"Please, just—" I broke down, to many memories flooded back into my mind all at once.

"Baby girl, I can see you're broken... But I can pick up the pieces, trust me." He kissed my lips and neck. But I shook my head no.

"No, this ain't me..." I repeated as I made him put me down and I ran like hell with tears streaming down my cheeks. I left him frustrated and confused. I couldn't be with him, even if he wanted to be with me.

***

Tyreese

The next day...

My phone rang and I thought this could be the call to change my life. Better yet, change my sister's life. I was tired of her working at that strip club. Duchess deserved so much better. Pacing, I was damn near about to burn a hole in the floor before I got the courage to answer the phone. "Hello, yes, this is Tyreese Moore." I said to the recruiter from the Lakers. My heart was thumping, and I felt like I couldn't breathe. "What? Please repeat that... *I'm* in? Yes, thank you so much!" I shouted.

I fist pumped my hand in the air as I was congratulated on the phone by the recruiter. Ever since my little sister sent me off to college, I've been making her proud now, because she didn't have to do what she did. Duchess could have kept her own money for herself. Or, tried to make her own life better. But she chose to do this for me, that's how strong our bond was. As a man, it was eating me up inside, but I can't believe I'm gone be drafted into the *NBA*! This was a dream come true, now I can take my sister out of the hell hole she's trapped in.

Thanking God for this blessing, I plopped down on the couch and was about to turn on the TV when I heard the key at the front door. I hadn't heard from Duchess since this morning when she left out, after she gave me this line about needing some space and air to clear her mind. So, I let her have it.

The door flew open, and she strolled into the house as she gave me a wave. Throwing the remote on the couch, I ran into my sister's room like a big ass kid.

"Sis!" She looked at me strange and laughed at my goofy face.

"Wassup, Reese? What got you so jittery?"

"Guess what?" I said smiling. Duchess threw her keys on the kitchen counter, made her way to the fridge and pulled out a water. Then turned back to me as she raised her eyebrow and cracked the water open.

"What?" Duchess asked.

"Well, that was my recruiter. I'm in, baby sis, I'm in!" I picked Duchess up and spun her around. When I put her down, her face expression wasn't as amused as mine was. And I realized it was the selfishness in me and I never thought of how this would impact her feelings.

"You're leaving, when?" Those words stung and hit the core of my heart. I promised never to leave her side and Duchess promised the same... and that's what I'm about to do.

"Y-yeah... but it's for us, sis. So, you can quit that damn job..." I followed Duchess as she walked to her room and sat on the bed, staring off into space, looking out the open window. I should have never sprung this on her, but something else got her feeling this way. I didn't know it was gone hurt her like this. It took a minute for her to finally break the silence.

"I'm proud of you, big bro. I really am... When are you going off to training camp?"

"Uh... So, about that. I actually leave next week..." Her mouth dropped and her eyes fluttered closed as she started to cry, her make-up started to run. "Sis... please don't, don't do that. I'm coming back..."

"No, you're not! You're leaving me like everyone else!" Duchess said as she cried and covered her mouth.

"But—" She ran off into her bathroom and slammed the door. I could hear her sobs. I really felt bad, but I knew even though she was mad at me, she wouldn't hold it against me for long. I had a plan to get out of here and make something of myself. Ball was my life, and I had the skills to get me where I needed to be. What got her like this? I dropped my head low. I just wanted our lives to be perfect, it was time for me to give back to my sister and all she's done for me. She needed to let me go... for both of us.

Chapter 6

Duchess

"Open up, sis... I'm not leaving you forever, just please talk to me," Tyreese said as he knocked on my bathroom door again. Ignoring him as the tears continued to fall, I sat on the bathroom sink. I knew this day was coming, just not this quickly. The fact that he was leaving, and I'd be alone, is what hit me the most and I just wasn't ready for it. I wasn't ready to be here in an empty space with no one.

I barely had friends, and the females I associated with, I didn't trust cause of the job I worked. There was no way we were hanging out or chilling at the crib. I just couldn't be in that dark place again. Depression is something else, and that was just somewhere I didn't need to be, again. I had to learn how to be by myself, but there was no way I was ready for that.

"Come on, Duchess, open the door. Please, don't act like that. I can't leave on bad terms. You think I want you here by yourself?" Grabbing some tissue off the roll and blowing my nose, I then balled up the tissue and dabbed my wet eyes. Sniffling, I looked in the mirror, to say I looked a hot mess was an understatement. Pulling myself together and taking a deep breath, I just wasn't prepared to be without my big brother.

Unlocking the bathroom door and opening it, Tyreese stood there looking sad as ever. Wiping my eyes as my make-up smeared and looking at him with puppy eyes, he opened his arms for me to hug him. Running to his arms like I was a little girl, I cried into his shoulder.

"You gone be okay. We gone be okay, sis. I promise and I'm sorry for springing this on you, Duchess," he said, while rubbing my back.

"It's just, we've never been apart like this. We've had each other's back since forever. You're my protector and I guess I look up to you, more like a father than a brother, and that's not fair to you. I can't keep you from your dreams. I did this for you, and I won't be selfish," I confessed as he rubbed my back in tiny circles. Tyreese sighed as he placed his chin on top of my head.

He took a deep breath and began to speak. "I know, and don't feel that way. I had to be there for you no matter what, I had to take that responsibility and I'm cool with that. Duchess, it's okay to be sad, but I know you'll be fine. I babied you too much and that's my fault. I didn't let you be who you needed to be, and that was me being overprotective. Duchess, I want you to be happy and fall in love one day. No way in hell I want you to turn out like Momma, sleeping with multiple men and out looking for love. It's your time to be happy and without your big brother in the way. So don't be mad at me, sis, it's been time for a change." I looked up at my brother as tears still fell down my cheeks.

"I know, I just had my moment." He hugged me tighter and all I could think about was how I'd handle this. We talked about him leaving, it hurt me to even talk about it. I needed Reese, who was my support. But now I'm on my own for now, had to learn how to do this by myself.

***

Later that night...

"Duchess, I'm going over bae house... I'll be back a little later, Nova will be cooking tonight. You want me to bring you something back?" he asked me as he popped his head in my room.

"Nah, but thanks for the offer. Tell Nova I said hi too," I said to Reese.

"You sure? She's cooking some ramen with bao buns, pork belly, and kimchi. I know that's your favorite too. She even gone have those sodas you like too," Reese said, trying to convince me. But I just didn't feel like eating, I knew how I got when I'm sad and trying to emotionally eat my problems away.

"Damn, she's putting that culinary degree to work! But I'm sure, Reese. Thanks for asking, really." He gave me a look but then shot me a smile.

"Okay, sis, it'll be late when I get back. Relax, I know you don't gotta work at the club tonight." I nodded and put my glasses back on as I read my book.

"Yeah, I'm glad, but have fun. See you later!" I said as he dipped out. I was going to try and enjoy my little relaxation time since I didn't have to work tonight. But I wondered if Yaheem would be there tonight and giving the attention he showed me to other women, especially the ones that knew he was throwing me racks.

"What the fuck am I thinking about him for?" I said, deeply sighing and rubbing my face as I shook off the thoughts of him and tried to finish my reading. But the thought of the events of the other day stormed into my brain. The way he kissed and felt on my body. It made me wet just thinking about it. Soon, I finally heard the front door close and lock, telling me Reese had left.

Closing the book, I just couldn't focus on right now, my mind was too clouded, I snuggled under my covers and turned on the TV. As I flipped through the channels trying yo find anything to watch. But I could feel my mind slipping off, thinking of Yaheem. My fantasy escalated to seeing Yaheem touching and kissing my body, just like he had done in the club. I found myself biting my lip as my hand traced down my titties to my stomach and then into my boy shorts.

Then his deep voice crept into my mind like he was right next to me and whispering into my ear. It turned me on so much and I found myself touching my wet pussy. "Come on, come on, baby... Cum on my tongue..." His words echoed in my head. Now it really felt like he was really in my bed between my legs right now. I moaned as his hands gripped my legs so I couldn't run away. It felt so damn real.

"Lemme taste you, Duchess..." he mumbled against my wet clit. I closed my eyes even tighter, so close to releasing. "Don't stop, Yaheem!" I moaned as I made my fingers go faster, continuing to imagine it was his long, wet tongue. My heartbeat sped up as I moaned more and more. But then someone knocked on the front door. They could go the fuck away, cause there was no way I was about to stop now, I was so close. The knocking continued and I almost jumped out of my damn skin. Trying so hard to ignore whoever it was, I was enjoying my alone time and damn near was about to squirt all over my sheets. "Fuuuck!" I yelled.

"You don't want me to stop hmmm..." I envisioned him saying against my area.

"Oh God, no!" I moaned as my back arched, and I almost jumped from my bed. Then someone began to knock on the front door hard as they could and rang the doorbell repeatedly. This was ridiculous and it was really annoying me.

I groaned aloud. I wanted to fucking cum already, I was just too close to stop now. Then I heard a male voice yelling outside the apartment front door. There was no way whoever that was, was going to leave. I groaned and became flustered. I had to get rid of whoever it was, cause this was just too much.

The knocking continued as I removed my fingers from my pussy, flung my cover back and swung my legs over the bed. "God dammit! What the fuck, man!" I yelled. "Hold the hell on!" I skipped into the bathroom to quickly clean myself. I changed my panties and washed my hands, and then put on my satin robe. I was so pissed off, I flung the bathroom door open and it slammed into the wall, damn near putting a hole in the wall. Walking out and into the hallway and stomping into the living towards the front door. At this point I didn't care who it was, didn't ask who it was, I just wanted to get rid of who it was. Opening the door, I instantly regretted ever unlocking it now. Cause the man who was in my face, I hated his damn guts.

"Wassup, Duchess? You don't know a nigga no more?" he said as he rubbed his facial hair and adjusted his hat.

"Keon, the fuck are you doing here? How you find out where the hell I live anyway?" I questioned him and adjusted my weight onto my other leg as I placed my hand on my hip.

"Well, I stopped by yo mama crib. She was rude as fuck but still told me where you stay." I couldn't stand her ass for real, cause why the fuck would she do that?

Rolling my eyes, I said, "I don't give a fuck. That didn't give you the right to pop up here. What do you want, Keon?"

"Man, never mind all that. Damn, you ain't miss me?" Before I could even say anything to his ass, he grabbed my waist and pulled me into his embrace. I inhaled his cologne, and the fragrance was so strong and sexual.

"Tuh, nothing like that." He gave me a mean look as he let me go.

"Why we fall off, Duchess? Come on! You gone do a nigga like that?" he whined. I hate when men do that female shit.

"Well, let's not forget it was my occupation, remember?" I said, trying to jog his memory. He sighed.

"Well, I ain't like all of them men staring at what the hell was mine. You'd rather shake yo ass for them than shake yo ass for me. I wasn't with that." I put my hand in his face.

"Uh-uh, save it! I don't wanna hear this, gone bout' yo business. Cause nigga, you a cheater, we both know that shit. You cheated on me the first chance you got, so please save yo shit for a bitch that wanna hear it," I said, standing my ground. Keon's face saddened, but I was serious. I had no time for his bullshit.

"Alright! Damn... But just know I really miss you... I came to get what we had back." I waved him off, I wasn't about to listen to his lies.

"Yeah, okay. Bye, Keon, don't slide to my spot no fucking more. Step." I closed the door in his face. I was mad, I lost all desire for what I was doing before I was rudely interrupted. The only thing I wanted to do now was sleep off my horniness. But it was too much, I just had to take a chance and go to the club. I just couldn't bring myself to do it right now.

***

Yaheem

"I'm lookin' paid and pretty (yeah)
Hair hanging down to my back, huh
I put it on him last night (woo!)
He calling me back to back, hey (hey)
Bitch this is a new outfit, huh (yeah)
Turn to the back for a pic, huh
Cognac Queen, I'm lit, woo!
Henn' dawg, Henn' dawg, Henn' dawg, Henn' dawg"

"Cognac Queen" by Megan Thee Stallion blasted in the club. This was my fifth night here, and now it was just getting out of hand. I know I'm a regular, but I'm getting looks and shit like I'm weird. And I'm the wrong nigga to get looked at sideways. Yo' head will be on a platter in five. Ion play that shit. I was really hooked on Duchess. And like I told her, she was what I wanted and needed.

Trigga strolled in with two bad ones on his arm. They looked like some bitches that was down for whatever for the right price. "Sup, mane!" he said, giving me a head nod as we dapped up. I did the same and kept on my bid'ness. I wanted to see her so bad. But I also needed my money from the niggas in the club, slanging to the hoes that needed they fix.

All I could wonder is if she was going to be here tonight. Duchess wasn't here last night and a nigga was out here acting like a crackhead over a bitch that wasn't even mine. Was she going to come on stage? Or not show up because what happened last night? I sighed to myself and sat on the soft leather.

Some ladies came through and sat on my lap, grinding on me, but it wasn't like how Duchess did it. But I wasn't about to let them not eat, I threw a couple of dubs, but they didn't do them tricks to get these racks. My attitude was up there, and I didn't even want the hoes on me. I waved them off, givin' them a few hunnids, to get rid of the hoes. One of them smacked their lips, I could tell they were pissed off, cause they wasn't getting that money or play like Duchess was. After I gave her a look, "You betta take that coin and walk the fuck off. Don't play with me, shorty," she gladly got out of my sight. I smoked just to get my mind off her but shit wasn't working. The twins came up on stage and they was doing they thing.

For some sisters, they did some real shit, kissing on stage got them extra attention. But, in my eyes it wasn't sexy. Where the hell is Duchess? I needed her, I wanted to pleasure her so bad. My dick got hard just thinking 'bout how she was moaning and talking. Just from my fingers in her. It had to be something in the damn liquor, cause her figure was bomb. The crowd was chill and a little live. They threw money but it wasn't really raining tonight.

I heard whistling and clapping, but it wasn't for the twins, it was for some woman switching into the club. Looked across the way and it was *Duchess*. I bit my lip while watching her smile and wave as she came through the spot. My niggas looked at me like I was crazy as I hopped up, following where she was going.

I quickly caught up to her, grabbing her arm softly. "Sup, ma?" She turned around and gave me a warm smile.

"Hi. What's up?" she said, nicer than last night. I licked my lips and grabbed her hips. This time, she didn't stop me.

"You mind if we talk?" I asked her. Her eyes glimmered and that shit made my dick even harder, her smile had a nigga's heart thumping.

"Yeah, sure, I don't work tonight. I'm just *here* for the vibes." If she had the day off, why was she here? Shorty had to be here to see me. *Maybe*. I don't know, maybe I was stretching.

"Okay, cool. Let's head to the back VIP," I said to her as I outstretched my hand for her to grab. She softly grabbed my hand and led me to a section. Not a private room, but somewhere in the back for VIPs only. She was being real nice, I don't know why. Maybe she smoked a blunt before she came here.

As we got to the back of the club where the lights were dimmed low, she asked me, "So, what you wanna talk about?"

"You," I said, looking her way as I took a puff of my blunt. She frowned.

"What about me?" she said with a slight attitude.

"Well, I wanna know, why are you here? A smart girl like you... Why?" I questioned seriously. She sighed. "Fuck it. Well, my mom kicked me out when she found out I worked at this club. Shit, all I was doing was helping her by doing this, but she didn't give a damn about me. This money is fast and easy, I got the body for it, and it was to make shit easy in my life. A lot happened to me as a child and none of my momma husband's kids never liked me but fuck them. You know, she had multiple men around us.

"My momma didn't give a fuck, she sold drugs and fucked multiple men. My pops died in the cold streets when I was seven. Only my big brother, Tyreese, did everything he could for me. We did live together, but he's moving away soon. With my money I earned from this place, I put him in college," Duchess said as she shrugged. "Things just happen." I knew it was something, but not like that. I knew it was more, but I wasn't going to pry.

"Damn, ma, that's some cold shit. For real," I spoke.

"Yeah, life is cold. But what about you? Why are you such a thug?" Duchess said.

"I been in this game a long time, you feel me? But it just some things I can't speak on yet. Things just happen... And this is my life," I said as I got closer to her. So close, I could smell her peppermint gum. "Answer this?" I bit my lip at how I was making her weak.

"I feel that and o-okay..." she stuttered out.

"On some real ass shit right now," licking my lips, "Are you wet right now?" I said with a smirk. She gasped and slapped my arm.

"No!" she spoke. I could tell she was lying.

"Come on. I said be real with a nigga. You can tell a nigga," I said with my full accent. "I know my voice gat ya' wet, ma... So, tell me, are you dripping? Or is that shit getting fat and throbbing—"

"Okay! Okay, I'm wet..." she said, flipping her hair and fanning herself. I knew I could make her cave.

"What you want me to do about that?" I said, looking her in the eyes. She quickly turned from me.

"I-I don't know..." she said timidly. I slapped her ass and gripped a handful of it. As she gasped and bit her lip, she looked back at me.

"Say what's on ya' mind and I'll do it," I said against her neck as I gripped it.

"I, fuck… mmm-hmm…" I cut her off as my hand slid up her tight ass dress and slid her thong to the side as I gently rubbed her clit, then put my finger in. As she moved her hips to me, I knew she wanted it.

"Say it, ma, go head, talk to me..." I said in her ear.

"Oh God, Yaheem… Mmm mmm, fuck me!" Duchess said as she moaned against my lips as she licked my lips. Music to my damn ears. I slid my finger out and she gave me a face that made me laugh.

"Not here..." I said as I licked my fingers, and she gave me a face again. I grabbed her face and kissed her deeply, her tongue explored my mouth and so did mine. "I'ma take you to my place, I don't wanna fuck you this fast. We can go get something to eat," I stated and she nodded.

"I'm cool with that," she whispered into my ear as she pulled me more on her. Her lips and tongue were amazing. I want and need to know what that mouth do.

Chapter 7

Yaheem

We pulled up to the Tenya Japanese Eatery, I had a thing for some ramen and sushi. And late-night sushi was so good. Especially when I was drunk, it just hit different. Personally, I didn't know if Duchess liked Japanese food, but we were about to see. "This is one of my favorite restaurants I ain't gone lie, I love some sushi. A nigga can be bougie sometimes too." I smiled.

Duchess looked at me with the cutest face. "Oh my God, I love Japanese food, that's one of my favorite foods ever. I love the hell out of some dumplings and bao buns. I can't believe you like sushi too! Never met a nigga who did," she said, turning and smiling at me again.

"No lie, I'm just a different type of nigga, ma," I said with a smirk. She waved me off with a laugh and shit, if a nigga can get a woman to laugh, he was in there. And soon enough I was gone have her.

"Well, let's see what you know about this food, boy." Before she could grab the car door handle, I grabbed her chin and pulled her face to me. My lips were so close to hers as I said, "One thing about me, I ain't no boy, shorty, I'ma man. And I'll show you too," I said as I bit her bottom lips. I could feel her body shiver as I left her wanting more. "Now you stay put, I'ma get the door for you."

"Okay," Duchess said, biting the corner of her lip. She stared at me as I hopped out of my whip. Adjusting my pants and my strap, I closed the door and came to her side, and opened the door for Duchess to get out. Grabbing her hand and helping her out the Maserati, I couldn't help but look at her perfect body as she switched towards the restaurant. That dress hugged every curve as she walked, Duchess looked sexy and classy in her outfit. Shorty could really dress, and it was nothing trashy about her. Her heels clicked on the pavement as I headed behind her.

The host greeted us as I swung my arm around her waist and pulled her closer to me. "Just a table for two." The host nodded and grabbed two menus. She looked into the restaurant as she spotted a table and booth, the packed restaurant was quite noisy. Rubbing her side with my thumb, we waited as the host came back around and directed us to come that way.

"Here's your booth and a waiter will be to you two soon. And by the way, y'all look like a lovely couple," she complimented as she placed our menus on the table. We both sat down. I looked at Duchess as she began to blush.

"See that, she thought I was yo man. Mmh," I said, smirking at her.

"Stop it, Yaheem," Duchess said laughing, nodding as I chuckled myself. I already knew what I was eating, but I also wanted to eat Duchess.

"So, what are you going to get to eat?" I asked her.

"Oh, I'm definitely getting the sushi platter and bao buns. Maybe I'll eat some of your ramen," she said, looking up at me.

"You gone eat my noodle, huh?" I asked with a smirk. Duchess laughed as she covered her mouth. I could feel her foot traveling up my leg, she didn't want to play these games with me.

"Maybe," Duchess said smartly. Just as I was about to say something, here came our waiter, asking what we wanted to eat tonight. As she was ordering, I grabbed her ankle and squeezed it softly as I gave her a look. I can tell she was trying to stay focused and she was doing a good job of it.

"Yeah, I'll have you guys' sushi platter, that does come with the California rolls, right?" she asked the waiter as I rubbed her ankle and then trailed my fingers up her leg as she cleared her throat.

"Yes, ma'am, it does. Would you like the wasabi and our secret sauce, along with the Japanese mayo?" he asked her while he wrote down everything.

I could feel her shudder before she spoke. "Yes, that's perfect and I'll also have the small platter of soup dumplings and pork bao buns. And for my drink, I'll take the sake and sparking soda water," she said with a smile as she passed him the menu. After he was done with her order, he turned to me.

"And for you, Mr. Carter?" I was a regular, so they knew exactly what I wanted. I rarely changed my food choice when I came here.

"The usual is fine, the dessert, I want the sweetest item on the menu. You guys know I'm not picky. Thank you," I said as I passed him my menu and looked towards Duchess, who looked shocked.

"Right away. I'll let the chef know, have a nice evening. I'll get those drinks and warm sake to you guys. My pleasure." I nodded at him and gave my full attention to Duchess.

"Oh, you just the shit, huh?" Duchess said as she giggled.

"Been the shit, ma. Now you need to stop playing games with me, heard me? Before I feed my sweet tooth early." I said licking my pearly whites and flashing my gold grill. My long arm was able to reach her thigh as I grazed my fingers over her pussy. Biting her bottom lip, she nodded and swatted my hand away.

"Okay, okay. But how does a nigga like you just come up like this? Huh?" she questioned me. I didn't say a word, cause the waiter was coming with our drinks. Soon as he sat them down and left, I looked her way as I took a sip of my soda water.

"Well, I learned from my older brother, Voshon. It was just the two of us. I seen how he stepped to niggas. How he moved in the streets. So, I took in his footsteps," I said, pausing and looking down. Duchess tried to find my eyes as I gazed up at her.

"And?" she said for me to keep talking.

"That's another conversation for another time, ma. I just want this night to be 'bout us. Cool?" She nodded with a smile as if she understood where I was coming from, which she did. Since she had told me about her losing her father. But at least she didn't have to see death, that was some shit I wish I'd never seen.

"We can do that. So, why are you single?" she questioned in this cutest voice, as she poured a shot of sake.

Laughing, I said, "Cause I haven't found the right shorty to hold me down, ma. But guess what?" I gave her my most toxic stare ever.

"What?" Duchess answered as she drank the sake down then chased it down with the soda water like a pro.

"I'm looking at her." Her eyes traveled up to mine and I had nothing but a smirk on my face as she blushed and moved her hair to the side. I had her right where I wanted her. As we continued to talk, the food finally arrived, we were both ready to eat. And I couldn't wait to be done with this so I could lick her entire body.

***

We pulled up to my crib and all I could her say over the music was, "Wow! This is your house? Damn, you are really living large! It's-it's so beautiful..." Duchess stated with excitement. I was living lavishly, I wasn't wasting my money and who cares if I was a hustler, at least I was spending it wisely.

"Not as beautiful as you though..." Duchess blushed as I turned the car off, hopped out, and opened the car door for her. Grabbing her hand, I led her to my front door and unlocked it in the process for us to go in. "Yep, this is my crib. Make yourself comfortable," I said, Duchess pulled off her heels at the front door, she was so short and tiny, I was gone manhandle the fuck outta her. Duchess was in awe as she looked around my house.

She made her way into the living room and sat on my huge plush sofa, still looking at all the black art I had, along with the art pieces around the house. I wasn't in a rush to get in her panties, it was the furthest thing from my mind, to be honest. But hell, I was still a nigga and needed her hands on me, especially those long nails dragging against my back.

"Why are you all the way over there..." She patted a seat by her. "Come take a seat next to me." As I turned on the seventy-two-inch flat screen TV, I could feel Duchess rubbing my leg and looking at me like she never seen a man like me before. She seemed so innocent. Why was she even in this type of industry?

"Why you lookin' all goofy like dat for?" I laughed as I mushed her head.

"Because I wanna play a game." I raised an eyebrow.

"What type of game, ma?" I asked as I looked at her then looked back at *Netflix* to find a show or movie. The cutest smirk played across her lips.

"Honestly, I wanna play Adult Uno, you got that? If not, we can just adlib with it," she said with a smirk.

"I ain't gone lie to you, I do have that shit. I swear, I do. Man, you a real down to earth female," I said to her as I got us to head into my game room to get it off the shelf. Once I got it, I went into my kitchen and got some Hennessy and Crown Royal too. I placed the game on the table.

"Definitely got the shit. I got some Hennessy and Crown Royal for us too. I don't know if you're a Henny drinker like me. But I got that peach Crown if you want that, shorty," I said to her as I stood there holding the drinks in my hands.

"I'll take the Crown. You got some soda to mix? Or I gotta drink it straight up?" Duchess questioned as she grabbed the game off the table and began to open it.

"Ma, you gone have to drink this straight up. If you can't hang, say that." Duchess smacked her lips and waved me off.

"Boy, I can hang," she said smartly.

"I told you about calling me *boy*. Set the game up so you can lose." I chuckled as I sipped the Henny I had just poured in a glass. I handed her a glass of Crown and sat next to her.

"I heard you, and I'm not gone lose. Here's your stack of cards, I already shuffled the stack," Duchess said, fanning out her set of cards.

"Bet." She motioned for me to draw the first card, so I did. I pulled my card and told her to drink or touch something private. Instead of drinking, she began to touch on my dick. "Yeah, nah, I see how this gone go."

"Well, touch my body..." she said, and I chuckled.

"I can do that with no problem." She nodded.

"Well, we need a blindfold," she said with a smile. The damn Uno game was over before it started the sexual tension was just too much. I sighed with amusement and got up to get my black and white bandana.

"So, you wanna go first or me?" She took the blindfold and tied it around my eyes. I wanted to go first, but I was glad she wanted to touch my body, because I damn sure wanted to touch hers.

"Okay... hmmm, what do I want you to touch first?" she said in a cute playful voice. "Oh, I got a good one."

"I bet you do..." She giggled and grabbed my hand. I heard rustling and laughed. She gripped my hand and placed it on something soft. "Now remember you can't touch too much, okay—"

"Girl, you must think I'm slow... That's your damn titty," I said with a grin, I squeezed it and she let out a little moan.

"I said, don't touch too much," she laughed.

"Okay, you next." I took the blindfold off and she ain't have her dress on. She was completely topless with nothing but a thong on. Yeah, that liquor had her feeling too loose. "Aw, damn..." I said, licking my lips like I was hungry. She was trying to start some shit, and I didn't want to give into her yet.

"Your turn..." My mouth was slightly open as I passed her the blindfold, them titties was so plump and perky. "Uh. huh..." I said with lust. She tied it around her head and her titties bounced at the same time. I got on hard in the matter of seconds, but I was trying to control it.

I grabbed her hand and extended her finger. As her long sexy nails pointed at me, I slowly put her finger in my mouth and pulled it out. "Uh... is that your tooth?" she said giggling, making her chest bounce again.

"Nah." I licked on her finger more and her smile turned into a smirk.

"That's your tongue, Yaheem!" I continued to suck on her finger as I rubbed my thumb on her hard nipple. "Mmm, Yaheem," Duchess moaned. Groaning, I pulled her finger out of my mouth and grabbed her thong as it clung to her hips. I pulled it off then picked her up in one swift motion. I pulled her in by her hips and put my wet tongue on her hard nipples as I twirled and sucked. "Shit, Yaheem." Duchess wrapped her legs around my waist, and I could feel her wet pussy soaking on my pants. She yanked off the blind fold and looked down at me.

"Enough of this damn game. You got me all on hard and shit, Duchess!" I said as I sucked on her titties more, then trailed my way down to her wet pussy. I placed her legs on my shoulders and lapped at her wet clit as I mumbled against her pussy, "But, since you wanna play, I'll do the same." I sucked on her clit and her back arched as I tasted her juices. I pulled away and licked my lips as she fluttered her eyes open and looked at me.

Pulling off my shirt and letting my chain dangle. I could hear the movie I put on was low in the background as I looked down at her and said, "Play with that pussy for me..." I said low and deep. She groaned with frustration and rubbed her little wet, fat clit.

"I did this earlier... Please don't tease me, Yaheem!" She begged me. That was going to make me fuck her harder, she'd played with it, without my permission.

"Oh shit, you got my dick hard." I unbuckled my jeans and pulled down my boxers. My long dick sprang free, making her eyes grow big. Then the excitement took over her.

"I want you to beg for it again," I said as I trailed my fingers on her wet pussy and I placed her juices on my dick, stroking it as I looked down on her. She slid off the couch and laid her body on my furry carpet and began to play with herself. I took one of the pillows off my couch and placed it under her head. As she toyed with her smooth wet pussy, I pulled out a condom from the side table and slid it on as I watched her.

"Come fuck me, Yaheem. Ohhh, I need you. I need that dick in me. Need you stroking me till I'm about to cum on your dick, Come lick on my pussy, baby..." She went fast with her fingers and her head dropped back against the fluffy pillow as her hand gripped the thick fuzzy fur carpet.

As she was begging me to make her body feel good, "Oh God, Yaheem, come on, I—" I moved her hand as her wet juices made a trail from her fingers sloshing around in it. Putting the tip in, moving in and out slowly as her moans grew louder.

"Nah, eyes on me!" Her hazel eyes landed on me, and she put her small hands on my waist.

"Nah, none of that shit. Move them hands!" Duchess moaned louder as I went deeper and pulled out, then went back in. Pulling it out and kneeling to suck on her clit.

"Fuck! Fuuuck, Yaheem!" Duchess moaned as soon as I began to suck and lick on her pussy.

"Hmmmm-mmm-hmm." I held her legs down as I hummed on her pussy, then stuck my tongue in giving her goosebunps. Her moans made my dick tighten.

"You gone cum for me?" I asked and looked up at her as I continued to eat Duchess alive.

"Yessss!" Duchess nearly screamed as her body shivered.

"Gone and do it then... Right now." I sucked on her clit harder and put my finger in. A combo that was going to send her over the edge. She started to moan out of control as she bit her lip and ran her hands through her hair. And at that moment, I pulled out my fingers and put my dick in. I stroked in and out, making her body shake while I felt her juices flow on my dick. Switching up my rhythm, I went into her slow, so slow, she begged me to go faster.

"Shit, please fuck me, Yaheem! I'm about to cum again!" I leaned down and groaned into her neck, and she clawed at my back.

"I am fucking you, ma, tell me what you want. Talk to me. I'ma take you to ecstasy. A ride of your life," I said deep into her ear.

"Uhhh, please go deeper. H-harder, Yaheem, touch my soul!" I smirked, because she knew I had more dick to give her, I wasn't even in all the way. Pulling out, she gasped as I flipped her over and watched her back arch like a pro. Working that pole really gave her some skills I'd never seen. Duchess started shaking her ass, I smacked it hard as I slid my dick into her tight wet pussy from the back. "Throw this ass back!"

"Fuck, daddy!" Got ha' calling me daddy already. I smirked and gripped her naturally long, black hair. And went harder and deeper from the back like she asked. "Ohhhh, fuck! Yaheem, I can feel you in my stomach!" she screamed. She started to run. But I wasn't done. I was far from done.

***

The next morning

I laid on the floor as the sun beamed in my eyes. Looking around all I seen on the floor was the empty liquor bottles, clothes, and condom wrappers. "Damn, man..." I propped myself up on my elbows, only to be alone in my house. Looking around, I called out her name. "Duchess, where you at, ma?" I shouted again. But no one answered. I rubbed my head and looked over at my couch, where a white note laid.

"Wow. The note shit." I sighed and picked it up, already knowing what it was about to say.

Went out to get coffee and breakfast. Since you wore both of us out last night. Will be back in a few. - Duch. I was shocked, I thought she had skipped out on a nigga. I laid back and put my hands behind my head. Maybe she was different from the others. I could tell I was falling deep for her. No way I was letting this one slip from my stronghold. I just laid there on the flooring, staring at the ceiling as I thought of what a simp she was turning me into. I needed her for a reason.

Chapter 8

Duchess

"Let me get one Grande Mocha Latte, no foam, with two pumps vanilla, and caramel. And one Grande Frappuccino with two pumps vanilla, and that'll be all." Making my order at Starbucks, I pulled up to the window and waited for the barista to take my card and give me my drinks. Once she opened the window and greeted me, I realized it was one of my momma's husband's kids, but I made sure not to pay it no mind, they didn't faze me. "I don't need to grab it, you can slide the card in, hold on, let me adjust it so you can reach it."

"No problem." Reaching slightly out the car window, I pushed in my Visa card and punched in the four digits.

"Okay ma'am, you can take the card out, and here's your drinks. Have a nice day!" She handed me my receipt and then passed over my drinks. Once I was settled in, I made my way back to his place, glad the Starbucks and Waffle House wasn't too far from his crib, I was not 'bout to deal with that Atlanta traffic.

I pulled into Yaheem's driveway and parked his car. I snatched his keys just to get us some breakfast while he was knocked out. I killed the engine and grabbed the coffee from Starbucks and our Waffle House breakfast. Mind you, it is nine in the morning, I'm an early bird so I don't even know if Yaheem is even up yet at this time.

His house was huge. I was going to explore this muthafucka, if he had a movie room, I was definitely going to watch any new movies he had. If he wasn't up, I don't think he read the note I'd left him before dipping out the crib.

I held one bag in my mouth as I tried to balance the other items in my hands. I opened the big door and stepped in as I kicked it to close the door. Yaheem was still on the floor sleep, like I expected. I put all the food plus the coffee on the countertop. His kitchen was huge, I looked around for plates, but it was so many cabinets and too many to pick from. Sighing, I picked up my Mocha Latte and sipped the hot coffee. I looked up because I felt someone watching me. But Yaheem's ass was still sound asleep. Shaking off the feeling and opening up his fridge to see if he had any fruit, I saw the only things he had in his fridge was some beer, carton of milk, and what looked like spoiled molded cheese.

"Damn, this man don't got no food..." I said, sighing.

"That's cause I'm hardly here." I jumped at his deep morning voice as he breathed down my neck.

"Shit, Yaheem! You nearly scared me to death!" I said, while clutching my chest. He chuckled and walked over to the food. Yaheem opened the Waffle House bag and pulled out a tray of sausage and opened it. He picked up one and took a bite as I looked him up and down, he was completely butt ass naked. Shit, I mean his dick was there looking at me, he was blessed as hell. I had to refrain myself from touching him or his booty as he turned to grab his Starbucks cup.

Shaking the feeling off he was giving me, I said, "Uh, yeah... so I got waffles, sausage of course, eggs, hash browns, and fried chicken. But I forgot the fruit." He nodded and gave me a warm smile as I watched while he took all the food out the bag and placed it on the other side of the countertop. Popping open another container, I grabbed a piece of chicken, taking a bite. I tried to grab my coffee but being so short and petite, I had to lean over the counter halfway on it to reach it. Reaching for it, Yaheem laughed and grabbed my booty, making me giggle.

"Short women are so cute," Yaheem said, I gave him a face.

"What?" he questioned as he studied my face,

"First of all, I'm fun-sized not short..." I said smirking.

"Mm-hmm got that right... Because I manhandled the fuck out of you and that pussy last night," he said, getting a view of my round butt. I paid no attention to Yaheem as I was trying to get some food, but Yaheem grabbed my elbow softly as he stopped me. "You so damn sexy..." I heard him groan as he pressed himself against me. He started kissing on my neck, making me bite my lip and nearly moan. But I stopped myself, I couldn't give into him that quickly. His hands roamed my body as his fingertips dragged against my exposed belly. Then his hand crept up to my titties and he squeezed one.

"You need to put on some clothes so we can eat..." I said giggling. "I'm hungry."

"The food can wait, ma... Come here." Yaheem kept kissing and licking on my neck and I tried to push him away.

"Yaheem, come on now, I'm hungry and need to eat, can you move your big dick out the way please..."

"Nah, I'm full of energy and I'm hungry for something other than this breakfast." He spun me around and kissed me deeply. His tongue made way into my mouth, and I couldn't help but wrap my arms around his neck. He groaned and picked me up as he carried me from the kitchen and put me on the bar stool on the other side.

"Mmmm... The food gone get cold... Shit, come on now, don't do this to me," I moaned out.

"We can heat that shit up later... This dick hard as fuck right now, I know you feel it. And he need some attention from that good ass pussy you got, girl..." He nipped at my neck and strongly ripped my dress I had on the other night. "I'll buy you a new one..."

"Dammit, Yaheem! That was a five-hundred-dollar dress!"

"I'll buy you something more expensive," he said as he sucked on my neck and kissed down to my chest. "Damn, I'm off them sweet juices nah." He leaned into my ear whispering in that New Orleans accent. "I know you remember, or do I need to refresh your memory?" He slightly lifted me up, as he stepped between my legs and pushed my legs farther open so I could feel his hardened dick more.

I threw my head back as his hand gripped my neck. "It's too early in the morning to be on hard, trying to fuck," I moaned out.

"Morning wood. Never too early, ma. You ain't know." He turned me around and bent me over the stool, getting a firm grip on my ass. Yaheem slapped my ass, and watched it jiggle back and forth.

"Fuck, Yaheem!" was all I could say when I felt his tip on my pussy lips. As he rubbed it up and down, I couldn't help but throw it back, trying to feel it inside me. Yaheem made me feel like no man could ever do.

"Yeah, do that shit again... I knew you wanted it as bad as I did." He gripped my waist tight as I threw it back. "Damn, you fucking wet... fuck, look back at me." I kept teasing and teasing, going back and forth in slow motion as I looked back at him. Yaheem's face was unamused, and he got tired of it. So, he pushed his dick all the way in. I gripped the seat as Yaheem stroked his dick inside of me.

"Mmm, fuck! Yes, yes, yes!" I moaned loudly. I threw my hand back on his stomach, trying to make him slow down in reaction, and he slapped it away.

"Didn't I tell you 'bout that shit? Don't make me hold you down and pound that pussy!" I moaned at his deep sexy voice as he stroked deep into me.

"Shit, baby!" I moaned as he sped up, going faster and faster by the minute. "Slow down, Yaheem!" I whimpered. He kissed my neck and went even deeper, causing my eyes to roll in the back of my head as he hit my pussy harder. He cupped my face as he kept doing that, until I felt this weird sensation in my stomach. Yaheem didn't stop as he stroked my G-spot and I squirted all over his dick. "Damn, Yaheem fuck, what the fuck! Don't stop, I'm cumming, aw shit, baby!"

"That ain't my name! What's my name? Huh?" he said, pounding faster and not stopping his rhythm as he reached under me and began rubbing my clit, which was making me moan uncontrollably. He was working me in ways I couldn't explain.

"Daddy! Daddy, ugh don't stop! That dick so big, keep going, keep going!" I screamed out in ecstasy. When he heard what I said, he went crazy. He scooped me up and pushed me against the wall, drilling into me as he pinned my legs against his shoulders and held onto me tightly. All that could be heard was my screams, my wet pussy, his grunts, and moans. This man was gone make me marry him.

***

Yaheem

I woke up to my phone ringing, grabbing and squinting my eyes at the name rolling across the screen. I answered it, "What's the word, Malachiah?" I said to my boy as he updated me on the trap. "They bagged all the dope? You and Justus made the drop, we got a lot riding on that shit. That's that big bank."

"Yeah, bro, Justus copped the bag. I just finished counting that shit. We made twice of what you asked for, my boy."

Rubbing my beard, I was satisfied with my product being sold properly.

"Bet, so did dude pay up at the shop, or I gotta handle that shit myself?" I inquired.

Malachiah sighed and I knew someone was gone get they head blew back by me if I didn't get my fucking money. "What! So, you mean to tell me Silas ass been ducking me? Nah, you and Justus don't even worry about that. I got his ass, they gone learn not to fuck with me."

"You got it, Yaheem. He gone be at the spot, he not even trying to hide out," Malachiah said through the phone.

I laughed. "Yeah, we gone see about that. But I'ma holla at cha. Be easy," I said.

"Be easy." Hanging up the phone and throwing it in front of me, I scoffed as I looked around the dark room "Where the fuck is Duchess?" I said out loud to myself.

Getting up, I flung the cover off me and picked my phone back up. Looking down at my phone, it was nine o'clock at night. The amount of messages and calls I missed was ridiculous. Missed calls from my boys and a text from Duchess, just one text. She went off to that damn club and I instantly became pissed.

At this point, I didn't want niggas even looking at her anymore, touching her, none of that! "Man fuck that shit," I said, storming into my bathroom and hopping in the shower. I didn't want her working there anymore, she didn't need to work there. Even though she wasn't my girlfriend, she meant a lot to me.

***

I walked into Diamond City iced out, looking around the joint, trying to spot Duchess. I rolled up on Bubbles. "Aye cuh, where Duchess ass at—" Before I could get the rest of the words out, she came out on stage.

"Throw them dollas for the queen of the pole, the royal flush, Duchess! And yeah... they say she *Taste Just Like Candy!*" the DJ announced as the beat of Lil Kim's hit song, "Taste Just Like Candy" began to blast in the club. Duchess rolled her body on stage as her colorful thong and bra exposed everything I had just seen hours ago.

Her colorful hair was flowing as she sported the same wig Nicki Minaj once wore in a music video. Our eyes met and she began dancing. The way she hit every move and touched her body, she wasn't dancing for none of these niggas, she was dancing for me. But I still wasn't having it. Her dance was the shit, but I didn't care. I waited till she got off the stage and I pulled her to the side.

"Hi, Yaheem—" she said as I grabbed her by the elbow and looked her up and down.

"Back room, now! And I ain't gone say it twice." I said in her ear, she knew I was angry by my tone.

"Mmmkay..." she said smiling as I gripped her hand and dragged her as she walked into one of the rooms before me. I shoved her inside and shut the door.

"You dead ass right now. No, for real, are you serious?" I said, grabbing her up by her throat as I spoke.

"Okay, what's wrong with you?" Duchess said, throwing her hands up.

"Why are you here tonight? You was with me not long ago and you back in this bitch! Why can't you quit doing this? Ion want my girl doing this!" She looked at me sideways.

"*Yo' girl?* First of all, when did I become your girl? We had sex, that's it..." Did she just think that was sex for me? I had some type of feelings for this woman.

"So, it's like that? You shaking your ass for other niggas when you was just bouncing that shit on my dick!" I said, grabbing her waist. She rolled her eyes.

"It's a job! I have stuff I need to take care of, Yaheem! We are clearly from two different worlds! Got two different paths in life." That's what she thought? Just because we came from two different projects, that shit didn't mean nothing. We both had fucked-up pasts.

"You wanna keep shaking your ass for cash, when all I'm trying to do is help! I can give you the lavish life, real fucking shit! Rolling up in nothing but minks and designers, besides Gucci and Louis. You won't have to want for shit!" I shouted and got closer to her.

"I don't need your damn handouts," she said coldly, shoving my hands away. "I got this, okay? We had sex and that's all it was ever going to be." I nodded and pulled her close to me.

"Ain't no nigga gone fuck you like I did... And that's some real shit." I grabbed her face and kissed her deeply. "Remember that shit, ma." I pulled away and walked out. I wasn't gone keep falling for these women only to get shitted on every time. She didn't need me, that was clear, and I didn't need her.

Chapter 9

Duchess

It's been a few weeks now and Yaheem meant what he said. I haven't heard from that man in weeks, and to say I was lonely was the least of my worries. He hasn't spoken to me, even when he's seen me in the club, he didn't look my way. Yaheem was even throwing money at bitches, getting lap dances and more. And I wasn't getting any of his attention. To make it worse, my brother was leaving today, how was I supposed to deal with that?

Tyreese scrambled around the house as there was a knock on the door. I don't know what made me think Yaheem would be at the door, but I speed walked to the front door and opened it with a smile on my face. But it was only Nova, Reese's girlfriend. She looked so sad in the face and my smile immediately faded.

"Hey Duchess, how you doing?" she said, trying not to sniffle.

"I'm doing the same as you, sad as fuck," I said, while stepping to the side so she could come in. Nova was a little shorter thanme with a short pixie cut that fit her small face. She was a small-framed female, not too skinny and favored Lil Baby's girlfriend, Jayda Wayda.

"I'm going to miss him so much. I really love your brother, Duchess," she said, wiping her eyes as I nodded. I knew she did.

"I know, I know you do. I'm so proud of him. But I can't see him leave, I just can't," I said honestly. She looked at me, and she could tell I was holding tears back.

"Duchess, I know how much he was there for you, but you at least have to see him off before he leaves. Really, you do."

She rubbed my shoulder. Sucking up my tears, I was not about to let her, or my brother see me cry.

"I just can't," I said to her as I looked out the window.

"You just can't what?" Tyreese said as he came out the back with his bag and suitcase in tow. The look on his face was of confusion and worry as he looked between me and his girlfriend. Sighing, I stood up from sitting on the edge of the couch.

"Well, Reese, I'm not going with you to drop you off at the bus. I'm sorry, but I just can't," I said to Tyreese. He looked at me and shook his head as he snickered a little.

"What, you mean you that mad at me you can't see me off before I leave? What type of shit is that, Duchess? Nah, I'm done with this shit."

"You're done? What? Reese, I'm sorry, I really am!" I said to Tyreese.

"Nah, I don't want to hear it. Duchess! You got a problem with yourself! You need to fix whatever is wrong with you, cause I can't do it! We have lives of our own and I'm going to live mine!" Tyreese yelled as he grabbed his things.

"Tyreese, wait!" I screamed at him. He grabbed Nova's hand as they walked towards the door.

"No, Duchess. I love you, but I got dreams. Come on, Nova, let's go. I can't miss this bus," he said, kissing her. Tears welled in my eyes as I watched him open the door and walk out, not even turning around to look at me.

Nova waved at me as tears fell down her cheeks and mouthed, "Sorry."

Once the door closed, I flopped down on the couch and cried, I knew I was in the wrong. The way I let my brother leave like that wasn't the right way to do it.

***

Later that day...

A couple of hours passed, and I was laying in my bed staring at the ceiling. All I could think of was my brother. I didn't hear from him, and he didn't tell me if his bus had made it. I had to hear it from Nova that Tyreese had made it. And here I was, thinking of Yaheem again. Maybe I was wrong for what I said and did. Fuck! I couldn't make up my mind. I don't know, it's not like anyone has fallen for me like this before. Finally getting up from my bed and walking to the living room, it was so empty and quiet in the house, I was trying so hard not to feel lonely.

Depression couldn't win this time. Running my hand through my long hair, I walked into the kitchen and went straight to the fridge. Pulling out a cream soda and half a deli sandwich, I sat at my counter and looked through my magazine as I ate. "Ari butt is entirely too big, fake ass. I hate fake bodies..." I said, rolling my eyes.

Flipping the next page, someone had a fabulous hairstyle and taking a bite of my sandwich, "Ohh, I love her hair color... I should dye my hair red," I said to myself as I scanned through the magazine. There was a soft knock on the door, and I sighed getting up. Who could this be visiting me? I sipped my cream soda before going to the door.

"Who is it?" I questioned as whoever it was knocked again.

"It's Keon," he said, I sighed and unlocked the door, then opened it. He stood there with his hands in his pocket as he looked up at me.

"Oh, hey...What's up, Keon?"

"What's up with you? I just wanted to talk... I really miss you, girl."

Yeah, just like I miss Yaheem.

"Okay, Keon, you can't just come over here unannounced and try to walk back into my life after what you did." He looked down.

"I know, but listen, it was a mistake. Can I take you out tonight?" I shrugged.

"Why, Keon? You cheated, you lied, what more can you do? Why try to make up after that, there's no coming back from that," I said, giving him a straight face.

"I know what I did was wrong, I'm trying to fix it, Duch. Come on, I know I was wrong for what I did. But I'm trying to be a grown man and come correct. Cheating on you was the worst mistake of my life. But you can't deny I was your first, Duchess, and—"

"And nothing. Just cause you was my first don't mean anything, you lost me when you cheated. So, good-bye, Keon." I closed the door and sat back where I was. I was just going to chill.

***

"Girl, come on, we're going out to dinner." I nodded, giving the twins a smile. I decided to finally go out and socialize. Why would I ever pass on good food, and plus I had no problems with the twins, they was cool people. I got dressed and went out with the girls. Just a simple dinner.

We made it to TGI Fridays and got seated, it was crowded in here. But I wasn't about to pass on some good ribs. The male waiter saw us fine women and seated us quickly. He wasn't a good tip, I could tell. "I'ma be fat and get me some ribs," I said as I sat down and flipped through the menu. "And, I'ma get a margarita or something else alcoholic."

"Girl, I want a fat burger and appetizer," Drika said.

"Girl, you already skinny," Leiloni said to her sister, I couldn't help but laugh.

Our waiter came over to take our drink orders. "I'll have a—" before I could finish my order, Leiloni hurried and pointed out something that made me freeze up.

"Girl, there go Yaheem and his crew..." the twins Leiloni and Drika pointed out as I turned around in my seat and saw him hugged up with some bitch. He was posted up with Justus, Trigga, and Malachiah. I know I shouldn't get mad, but I was jealous. She was all up on Yaheem and kissing on him. The green eye was all over me.

Forgetting all about the food, I got up and walked over to his table cause I didn't give a fuck, I needed answers. "So, this what we do now?" I said, putting my hand on my hip. He deeply chuckled as I stood there staring him and his hoe down. His niggas and bitch were staring at me like I was crazy.

"We ain't together. Gon' by ya' bid'ness," he said, waving me off.

"Yeah bitch, leave," his hoe said, sipping her drink. It took everything in me not to drag her around this restaurant, but I wasn't about to cause a scene.

"Hoe, no one was talking to you. Stay in yo' pussy ass lane," I said. His boys got to cracking up as she didn't say a word. "Mm-hmm. Yeah, I'll leave you to being with your hoe." I turned around and went back to my table, not saying a word.

***

Yaheem

After seeing Duchess at the restaurant, I ain't feel bad at all. She dubbed me and thought she could question me about what I was doing, nah. But I did miss the girl, that wasn't a lie. Shid, she ain't want a nigga, so it's whatever. She made that shit very clear at the club that night.

"Yaheem, why you so distant?" the girl questioned. I didn't even know her damn name.

"Nothing..." I said dryly. She climbed on top of me and started kissing on me and trying to go down on me.

"Shorty, if you not gone top me off, get the fuck off me. I don't even know you like that. The hell is your name again?" I said, pushing her away. I wasn't the one to push females away when it came to this, but I wasn't feeling her at all.

"Whatever, when you wanna fuck call me up." I shrugged as she grabbed her things and left.

"Ha, I will never call you, shorty. You know where the door is. I ain't want you anyway..." I checked my phone to see what time it was. It was 11:45 p.m. I had shit to do, and I had to roll up on that nigga Silas. Getting up from the couch, I jogged up to my room and got dressed in all black. This nigga owed me money and I was going to get my shit. Ringing up Trigga, he answered on the fifth ring. I could hear him cracking some bitch on the other end.

"Aye, meet me at the spot, finna roll up on Silas punk ass and get my shit," I said to Trigga as I strode out the crib and to my Benz.

"Aye, lil mama, hold up. And cool, bro, I'll be down that way in five. I'll be pulling up same time as you, my boy," he said as I could hear the girl begging him to stay, I shook my head.

"Cool, be easy," I said as I hung the phone up and hopped in my truck and sped off to the barbershop. This nigga was gone see what the fuck I was talking about. He thought he was slick. What was loaned from me was going to be paid back or hell was gone break loose. Weaving through Atlanta traffic, I pulled up to the shop in thirty minutes flat, and Trigga pulled up not a minute later. I got out my Benz and Trigga dapped me up. "Finna straighten this shit out."

Walking into the shop, it was a few niggas getting shaped up. There was a fine ass jawn doing a fade, her ass was fat so I know they was getting hellafied money from her alone. So, he couldn't lie about not being able to pay up. I gave Silas too many chances and this was the finally straw.

"What's the word, shorty, I need shape," I said to the bad jawn who was taking care of a customer. She looked up at me and was damn near drooling.

"Damn, I mean… yeah, I can take care of you. I just finished him up. Pay the rep, baby boy, and thanks for the tip," she said to her client before looking me up and down. "I'm Fancy, yo dreads are on point, but you do need a slight edge up. Come take a seat, I got you." Fancy patted the barber chair. I sat down as Trigga stood next to us. She knew exactly who he was, so she didn't say a word. Fancy pulled out her clippers and began to edge me up.

Soon as she started, I heard Silas from the back. Trigga knew just what to do. He didn't want him to run out the back, we didn't have time for a chase. So as Silas was laughing and some more shit. He came out of his office with some female on his arm.

"Baby, when I'ma see you again? I'ma need what you was giving me in the back again," she whined to Silas. But before he could answer her, I did it for him.

"You'll probably never see him again. Shorty, I suggest you give him a kiss and gone up outta here. Matter a fact, everyone can dip, except you, Fancy. You ain't done," I said as she nodded and continued to finish me up, but I could feel her shaking. "No need to be frightened, ma, relax. I don't want my line-up fucked up," I said, looking up at her slightly. She nodded without any words.

"So, Silas, how you been, my nigga?" I said smirking. The girl caught the drift and dipped out before he could say anything to her. Trigga maneuvered around so Silas couldn't run out the back like a hoe nigga.

"Man, I been chill. What's up, dawg?" Silas said, trying to grow some balls.

"*What's up?* Man, everyone out this bitch, like I said! Moving like y'all got a hearing problem! Leave right the fuck now!" I yelled. Everyone knew what I was about and scrambled out of the shop. "Now, like the fuck I was saying." Fancy's clippers stopped and she handed me a mirror. I looked at my line up and this shit was fresh as fuck. "Damn shorty, you good as fuck." Reaching in my pocket, I gave her a grand, and instructed her to slide in the back room. "Don't come out till I say so, cool?" Fancy nodded and moved fast in them heels. She knew the vibe, I could use her for my personal shape-ups, no doubt.

Brushing the hair off me, I put my attention back on Silas. "Now, like I was saying. Fuck is my money, bro? And I ain't playing, you thought I was the one to play with? Me, Versace?" I said, rolling my neck and shoulders as I stared him down.

"Man, I don't owe you shit. This my spot I run this 'round here." Trigga stepped up and hit him with a shot to the ribs.

"Ah! What the fuck!" he yelled.

"Speak correctly before you lose yo' fucking tongue!" I yelled, "Now where the fuck is my fifty thou? Either run my shit or you know what's gone happen. You know about me, so why play with yo' life?"

"Fifty thou! I only borrowed twenty thousand!" Silas shouted.

"It's called interest, bitch nigga," Trigga yelled in his ear. "Run me my money, Silas. This the last time I'll ask nicely. Shid, you lucky I'm this nice," I said as I looked at my Rolex to check the time, Trigga slid on his brass knuckles. "Trigga, what time you got, my boy?"

"Quarter after beat a bitch down," Trigga said with a smirk.

"Yo, Versace, I'm not running you shit! I don't owe you nothing. This my place of business!" he yelled. I just laughed in his face.

"Oh, you thought you just ate, huh? Ight, ight. Trigga, you know what to do." Trigga cracked Silas in the jaw with the brass knuckles more than once as blood trickled down his mouth. He tried to touch his jaw as he was in shock, but I slapped the fuck outta him.

"The fuck, man! Okay!" Silas yelled.

"My money, now," I said through gritted teeth.

"You ain't shit, fuck you! You think just cause you're Joker's brother you run shit, you nothing but a bitch!" Silas yelled as he spat blood on me. Freezing up in the spot I stood in, Trigga looked at me as he saw the rage take over. Grabbing him by his shirt, I wiped the blood off my face. Pulled my Glock from the back of my pants and pointed it in his face. Pointed it dead in his eye, cause who was he to speak on my dead brother's name?

"Fuck you say to me? Bitch, don't you ever speak on my blood brother like that again. Don't ever speak his name. You know what, I should kill yo bitch ass right now. Fuck this, nigga! I'll put a bullet in-between your eyes right now, bitch! Fuck is my money, I'll splatter yo shit all over this mutha-fucka!" He began crying like a little bitch.

"I'm sorry! Listen! Okay! Please, I got a safe in the back, all the money is there, I swear! I swear to God, all yo' money and then some is in there!" he screamed as I kept the gun in his face.

"Yeah, and just so you know, I own this bitch now." He nodded and Trigga stood him up from his knees. "Oh, yeah."
Pow! Pow!

I shot him in the leg and knee twice as he screamed. "That's for speaking on my brother. You'll never walk right in this bitch again. Now go get my money, bitch ass nigga!" I called Fancy in and told her she'd be working for me now. Nigga's been playing with me, I had to step on nigga's neck, I bet a bitch nigga won't try me again. They knew who the fuck I was.

*****

Soon as I pulled back up to my crib and poured me up a glass of Hennessy, before I could even drink it, there was a knock on the door. I just thought ol' girl was trying to get some dick like she said earlier. She wasn't going to get any of that, I didn't want any bitches right now. I got up, pulling up my pants and drinking my drank as I went to open the door. Before I could say anything, she attacked me with kisses, while tangling her hands in my long dreads.

Duchess was something I just couldn't deny even if I tried to. I wanted her so bad anyway. Picking Duchess up, I pressed her against the front door, closing it. She said in-between kisses, "I felt salty as hell seeing you with that hoe. I want you to myself. I'm sorry for what I said, daddy."

"Show me you're sorry. Right now, Duchess." She pressed her lips into mine. Pushed me off her as she hopped down. I didn't know what she was about to do to me, but I wouldn't mind. Duchess grabbed my hand as we walked to my bedroom and pushed me back on the bed as she yanked my pants down. With my drink still in my hand, I gulped it down. The glass rolled out my hand as she pulled out my dick and her tongue lapped all over me and worked like a pro. Her spit rolled down my dick as her mouth drooled all over me.

Licking my lips, I watched as Duchess licked it like candy and rolled her neck, as she sucked and rolled her hand on my dick. "Let me serve you up, daddy. Relax," Duchess said as she kissed and licked on my dick like she loved me. The slurps she was making as she sucked me made me grab her hair, this was something I never expected out of Duchess. I never nutted off head. But the way she was working her mouth made me think this was the night my dick was gone buss in a shorty mouth.

"Do yo' thang, ma." I placed my hands behind my head as she was working that mouth on me. She trailed her hand up my stomach, I could feel her tongue twirling around the shaft of my dick, and she popped my tip in and out of her mouth. She moved her hand from my dick and began massaging my balls as she throated my dick with no hands and spit began to go everywhere,

"Mmm, you taste so good, daddy." The next thing I knew my whole dick was in her throat as she was gagging and swallowing me up. Duchess don't think I'm finna beat this shit up to where she can't even walk tomorrow, but she sadly mistaken...

"Oh, daddy! I'm sorry!" she screamed as I pounded into her guts, trying to touch her insides. She was getting this dick like I never gave it to her before.

"Uh huh! That's what I thought, running 'round here like you crazy. Talking all that shit, now look at you, creaming on my dick! Thought you could stay away, huh, Duchess? Now who pussy this is?" I groaned.

Duchess was moaning into the pillow like fuck as I was digging that pussy out. "Oh daddy, it's yours! This all yours, baby!" she screamed as I pulled her face out the pillow by her hair.

"It better be, Duchess! Your all mines na'... Rememba' that. This all you wanted me fo was to fuck that pussy up, huh?" Letting her hair go, her head fell into the pillow as she tried to push me back. I wasn't showing her no mercy this time. "Yeahhh, what I told you bout that, c'mere," I said as I grabbed her hands and beat that pussy up more till she was gushing and that pussy was clapping her juices all on me.

"Oh my God, daddy, slow down! Baby, shit!" she moaned out. I could feel her cum squirting back on my dick. Damn, she got that good shit.

"Damn, Duchess, you tryna make me bust so I can slow down? You gotta try harder than that! You made me nut from that pretty mouth, now you gotta work for this nut!" I groaned. She backed her ass on my dick hard and arched her back so good. Slapping her ass a few times, I released her hands. Duchess reached under her and rubbed her pussy and my balls at the same time.

She was working this dick and I slowed my strokes in her pussy while feeling my dick tighten up in her. I felt my warm cum shot out into the condom as her body began to shake and her pussy gripped me repeatedly as her pussy squirted once again, Duchess started to edge off my dick, but I quickly gripped her hips tightly and slid my dick all the way deep as she screamed to the top of her lungs, "Fuck, girl, stop fuckin' running." I had a death grip on her hips and went faster and harder. So deep, I was hitting her G-spot once again.

"Shit! Shit, Yaheem, I'm cumming again! Fuck!" I laid on her back, holding her hands in mine, going so slow and deep as I was breathing heavily on the back of her neck. In a matter of minutes, I let all my cum fill the condom up. I pulled out and kissed down her back as she shivered under my touch. I slid the condom off and groaned at the sensation. Duchess moaned and it was just turning me on more. So, I glided my fingers over her sensitive pussy to make her try to push me off. "Yaheem, ohhh shit!" she said soft and sexy.

"Damn, ma." I smacked her ass and began to eat her out from the back.

"Shit, Yah! Give me a break! Baby, please."

"Uh-uh nah, you was trying to get rid of me... I ain't lettin' up till you cum in my mouth." She groaned in pleasure and tried to push my head away. But she was so weak as she started to shake again. I stuck my tongue in her wet pussy, and she began to moan over and over as she gripped my dreads.

"Babyyyy! Fuck! Huhhhh!" I was gone do this shit all night long.

***

Keon

"She just turned me down, my nigga. I tried everything and she didn't give me one chance," I said to my nigga Trigga as we smoked on my porch. We go way back, and he was my homie, so I had to get some kinda advice.

"So man, what you gone do? You did cheat on her with her best friend. That's some dirty shit you know, females don't get over shit like that. Besides dawg, you may be outta luck. I heard she kicking it with my nigga Versace, mane, you need to stay away from her. He don't play about shit like that. He a trip when it comes to his. So, leave her alone, bro," he said, blowing smoke as he looked at the blunt like it was the best he ever rolled. Then I thought, *that's why she was ducking me, cause of that nigga Versace.*

"Man, fuck you talm' bout she was mine from the beginning? I know what I did, don't fucking remind me... she can't just let a relationship like we had go like that. I used to spoil that girl, give her everything she wanted. All she had to do was stop working at that damn club, that's all I asked," I said, straightforward.

"Man, that's not all you asked. You accused her of sucking and fucking some ole nigga she didn't even know. He was just a regular at the club. I remember everything you tell me, nigga, so stop lying. And since you big and bold... Tell that shit to Versace..." I shot him a look and snatched the blunt from him and took a puff. Trigga laughed as he blew the smoke into O's. I wanted my woman back. And I was intent on getting her by any means necessary. Even if that meant fuckin with Versace.

Chapter 10

Yaheem

I felt shifting next to me and honestly, a nigga was trying to get some shuteye, I had shit to get done later in the day and the sleep I needed to have, had to be at least eight hours' worth. "Aye mama, quit all that shuffling with yo' feet, man..." I huffed as I laid on my back. Sliding my hand in my shorts and holding my dick, I put my arm over my eyes.

Duchess said in her soft voice, "Yaheem, I can't sleep." I ignored her.

"Come on, now. I'm trying to sleep for real, Duchess, just tell me in the morning," I said as I sighed.

"Yaheem, I know you hear me. And who sleeps like that?" Duchess said to me as she smacked her lips.

"A real nigga," I said, Duchess was stressing me out for what, cause I was tired as hell.

"Well, nigga, you nasty..." she huffed.

"Wasn't saying that shit for the last couple of nights. Don't make me fuck you up again, Duchess. Damn, now what chu' want, girl? Fuck, I'm up now."

"This is just so weird to me. I don't know, I think we need to be friends or something. I love being around you and all... But I'm not ready for no relationship yet..." I raised up from the bed and looked at her sideways.

"You joking, right? After what we did and talked about. You gone flip-flop on me again? What game are you playing, Duchess, *see how many times you can ride my dick?* I'm trying to give you a better life and be yo' man! What else you want me to do? What?" I said, growing angry.

"It's nothing like that, Yah... I've been hurt so many times before and I don't know if I can trust easy again." Listening to Duchess, I sighed.

"Just let me understand this. So, letting me put my dick in you, that's trust, Duchess? Every night you been at my crib, we been fucking! Duchess, I've been trying to take care of you, and you've been brushing that off. But when it comes to fucking, that's easy for you. Man, I don't understand you. If you just wanna be friends, then coo'. I ain't gon' beg but this long dick between my legs is off limits to yo' ass. Fucking friends is something I don't do," I said, turning over.

A nigga was beyond confused, one moment it's, *"I want you to myself, Yaheem. Now it's, I wanna be friends?"* Shorty gotta make up her mind or I'ma be outta her life for real.

"Yah, you just don't get it. But you'd really hold out on me?" she said, kissing my neck and ear.

"Man, Ion wanna hear it, now go to sleep, *friend...* All these games you playing and shit." She smacked her lips and turned over without a word. "Smack yo' lips again, Duchess, I ain't in the mood to play with you." She huffed and turned back over. *I just can't believe she wants to be just friends, fucking friends!* The way Duchess is going back and forth makes it seem likes she's just using me. She not that kind of girl to me. But she pushing it.

***

"Yaheem, I'm leaving out!" she yelled from downstairs. I continued to play *2K* on PS5, what she was talking about, I didn't care to hear.

"Yop..." I said, laying in the bed as I won my court session. As I was about to run another one, I could hear her footsteps jogging up the stairs. Then the door opened, and she stood there with her hands on her hips.

"I can't get a hug or none?" she questioned with her baby voice. She knew I was still mad at her. And I wasn't about to feed into her mess.

"Nah, Duchess, friends don't hug." She huffed and left out the door. I just wanted her in this bed calling me bae and shit. But she was on some bullshit I wasn't going to feed into. A nigga ain't bad and I'm damn sure not gone cheat on her. Duchess just don't see that I can be a good guy. Gave her everything she ever desired, loved her like she wished, and wined and dined her like she needed to be. Despite me being a hustler and all.

I heard her Hellcat pull off. Scoffing, I just finished what I was doing. A nigga dick was all on hard too and all I wanted was her pretty lil mouth on it. And begging for me to be with her, but that's all she seems to want. Shit ain't coo'. Instantly becoming irritated, I threw the controller to the side of me on the bed. I closed my eyes and fell asleep quick, shid, a nigga was tired.

My eyes got super heavy as I dozed off. "What the fuck goin' on?" My door slightly opened and the sexiest woman strutted into my room. Her light brown skin legs were long and smooth, and her curves were to die for. It was Duchess...

She stripped out of everything and crawled to me, looking like a vixen. Long black hair pulled into a ponytail, with black lipstick on her lips. She licked those plump ass lips as she made her way to my dick.

"Daddy, I'm sorry for being a bad girl... You forgive me?" Her wet tongue swirled around the head of my extremely hard dick.

"Uh-huh... You know I do." She smirked the freakiest look ever and took me all the way in her mouth. I groaned at the sensation.

"Shit, Duchess, I love you..."

"Mm-hmm..." She began to go fast and the lights went out in the room. But then she vanished, and Duchess was dancing on my dick. Literally. She was butt ass naked and just bouncing on me.

"Ahh, daddy!" I couldn't handle this shit no more. I grabbed her by her luscious hips and began to drill into her. Hearing that lovely sound of her juices on my dick, I groaned as I was about to buss the fattest nut ever, then my eyes shot open.

"The hell? Aw, damn!" I looked at my dick and I busted a nut over a wet dream about Duchess. I fell back on my bed and ran my hands down my face. "Why she gotta be cold to a nigga? Fuck! Could be here kissin' and suckin' a nigga off," I mumbled as I got up from the bed. I made my way into my grand bathroom and cut in the shower on. Instead of being here alone, I had shit to do. "Another damn cold shower fa me," I grumbled as I pulled the door back and stepped in. This shit irritating as fuck. After this, I had to slide to the trap. If being in the streets was going to keep my mind off her, then that's what it was going to be.

***

After hopping out the shower, I left the crib and headed down to the trap to meet up with Justus. He had to tell me about this nigga who was snubbing out the females at the club over drugs. He was a fiend for pussy, and he was pushing drugs in my territory. I know damn well Miss Coffee didn't approve of that shit. He let me serve, cause I gave his club extra funds and protection from anyone who tries to do some fuck shit.

So whoever this was, Miss Coffee didn't know he was pushing drugs there, soon as I found out, shit was gone get real hectic.

***

Duchess

"Another day, another dolla'" I said to myself as I came in with all my cash.

"Look who strolled in the room, Ms. Suck-A-Dick..." Candice, aka Babi Blu, said as I sat at my dresser. Don't know who the fuck this bitch was, talking to me like that. But I was bored with her shit.

"Fuck you in my seat for? Get the fuck up, I don't know what tha fuck you talm' bout but you can miss me with the bullshit. Not for your shit hoe." I stated firmly rolling my eyes.

She chuckled. "Everyone in this damn place know you sucked Yaheem Carter off in the back room. Bitch, we all know you ain't no goodie two shoes, you a hoe like the rest." I snapped my head at her. I was sick of the bitch, don't even know what she talking about.

"Hoe! Get you facts straight, you blueberry lookin' ass hoe! I ain't suck no dick for cash. You shouldn't be the one talkin' wannabe Pinky ass. We all know you the biggest slut here, you suck everything with a dick, bitch. You fucked every nigga you gave a dance to for extra cash. So, get off my pussy, you cum-bucket. Before you wanna start drama, I suggest you move along with your Grand Puba lookin' ass. Bitch I know that ass is fake, you over there looking like a blow-up Nicki

Minaj. Go somewhere and get them ass shots like you do every time you get paid, cause boo, yours will never be real like mine... Clean up yo leaky ass."

I flipped my real hair and turned my back on her, but this hoe wanted to get feisty and pull my hair. I turned around and got to swinging off on her ass. Not missing one punch to her ugly face, I chin checked her. My brother taught me how to fight, so she fucked with the wrong one on the right day.

"You stupid muthafucka! You dumb bitch! I'm tired of you, sloppy ass hoe! Muthafucka!" All the ladies were screaming for me to stop, but I was tired of the disrespectful shit. Bubbles and the other bodyguards came in and yanked us apart.

"You betta watch yo' back, hoe! Mark my fuckin' words, bitch!" Candice yelled as they removed her from the room.

"Yeah, bitch! Go fix your face, you bleeding bitch! I left you leaking, bitch, what's good! What's good! You fucked with the wrong one, boo!" I snatched away from the body-guards and fixed myself. I had a minor cut on my lip. But I did worse to Blues Clues over there. Shaking it off, I got dressed and grabbed my stuff as I walked out the room.

I didn't see Yaheem, which kind of made my heart drop. Maybe he just didn't want to see me tonight. I sighed and walked out to my car. It was darker than usual, so I wanted to hurry up and get to my vehicle. Bubbles usually walked me out here, but since they were dealing with her crazy ass, I had to walk out here by myself.

I dropped my keys on the ground when I got to my car door and cursed myself for it. "Dammit!" I huffed while I picked them up. This uneasy feeling came over me, when I put the keys in the lock, I felt someone grab me roughly.

"Marco! What the fuck?" He had the most sinister look on his face.

"You gone give me this fucking pussy! Bitch, you knew what you were doing when you played me! Led me on, so what if it was a one-night stand! You made it seem like we had something, bitch!" I tussled with him. I was not about to be raped, not ever again. I kneed him in the balls and watched as he crumpled to the ground.

I tried to hurry and get in my car, but I was shaking so bad my fingers were trembling. But then I froze when I felt him something cold against my back, a gun. "Shit! You stupid bitch..." he screeched. He turned me around and pulled my hair, yanking it at the roots as he shoved the gun in my face. Never in my life has a gun ever been buried in my cheek.

"Marco! The hell is wrong with you! Come on now, be cool, you don't gotta do all this!" He put the gun to my neck and my body never froze so quickly. "Please, just calm down."

"Yeah? Why so quiet now, huh? Bitch, where was all that mouth?" Marco said as I looked away in fear.

"Please—" He shoved the gun deeper in my neck and immediately I stopped talking.

"Shut up! Now you gone give it to me! Run me them keys, bitch, I'm not playing!" Pushing him my keys, he put them in my door and unlocked it. He quickly shoved me in the back seat, still pointing the gun at me. I wasn't about to die tonight, so I did everything he said. He climbed top of me and repeatedly hit me in my stomach, face, and ribs till I was screaming for help from anyone to hear me. Marco got tired of my screams and shoved the gun back in my face.

"Bitch, shut the fuck up! I'll shoot you right now!" I whimpered as the tears ran down my cheeks.

"Okay, okay..." His tongue dragged across my face, and I closed my eyes, wishing it was over. I wanted to scream, but the music booming from inside the club was perfect cover, and

I didn't want a bullet in my head. Marco grunted as he un-zipped his pants and pulled his dick out. My lips quivered as my heart thumped in fear. I felt his dick against my leg as he ripped my leggings and panties.

Marco held me down as he kept the gun pointed my way. And then I felt it against my pussy, only Yaheem has been near it, I belonged to him. I wouldn't be in this situation if I'd just listened to him. I wish he would come and save me! Marco ripped off my clothes and my fight was over. I felt thirteen years old again.

"Yeah! You like that, uh-huh!" he growled, and he shoved himself in me. I screamed in pain. "Yeahh... shit, girl!" He pumped harder as I wailed. It felt like this was going on for hours, but it was just minutes of me crying and screaming. Tears slipped down my eyes but then the car door flew open, and someone snatched him from the car. "Fuck!" Marco yelled as he hit the ground.

I heard pounding and bones crushing. I wiped away my tears as I backed away in fear into the fetal position against the closed door.

"Duchess, come on grab my hand. You okay now, baby girl, c'mon... trust me. Take my hand," Keon's faint voice filled my ears. And as I praised God he showed up, I reached out and grabbed his hand as he pulled me from my backseat. I covered myself as he held me close. His niggas were beating the brakes off Marco. And all I could do was stand there in shock as tears stained my cheeks.

Some laughter came going towards the club, and I looked over Keon's shoulder to see Yaheem and his crew walking up to the club. Marco's loud groans caught his attention and when he looked towards this way, he stopped in his tracks and Yaheem's eyes locked with mine. "Yo, what the fuck!" Yaheem yelled as he ran over to where I was, with his crew right behind him.

"Duchess, what the fuck happened?" I ran to Yaheem as I cried and wailed. He quickly took his shirt off, throwing it over my head to cover my body.

"This nigga tried to rape her..." Keon stated, looking at us, as Trigga kicked Marco in the ribs till the sound of bones cracking filled my ears. Yaheem looked at him good. He snatched him up and shoved him against the car.

"Aye man, I didn't ask you, bro!" Yaheem yelled at Keon. "Duchess, baby, this nigga did that shit to you!" I nodded without words. I just couldn't say it. And the look on his face, I never seen him like this, ever. "Nigga, you touched my girl, bitch! Are you dumb!" He punched him in the face hard and he spit out blood.

Then Yaheem looked at Keon with a confused face. "Nigga, how the fuck you just show up outta nowhere, Keon? Don't this nigga run with you anyway? I was coming to check this nigga about selling at this club, and he sell yo shit! I think this some bullshit!" I looked at Keon and he shook his head no.

"Nah, man, I'd never do some sick shit like that, bruh!" Keon yelled in his own defense.

"You set-up my girl!" Yaheem screamed, causing me to jump in fear. "Huh!" Yaheem yelled again as he kept a tight hold on Marco's neck.

"Nah, mane! We just seen this shit happen..." Keon said with his hands up. "Trigga, this shit is fucked up!" Yaheem yelled. But Yaheem and Keon looked like enemies.

"I know, bro, fuck you want us to do with this nigga, since he wanna touch on shit that don't belong to him."

"Take this nigga to the docks. Make sure he'll never be able to use that muthafucka again. Since he wanna rape folks, he won't breathe another god damn day! Make sure this nigga suffers till his last breath." Yaheem slung him to his boys. "Wait a minute... Let baby girl get a hit in on his ass," Yaheem offered, and I was glad to do so. I skipped over to him and kicked him repeatedly in the balls. "Bitch!" I screamed as Yaheem pulled me into his arms.

They took him away and all I could do was cry. This was a wake-up call for sure. "Duchess, I swear on my life, I ain't set you up! You gotta trust me," Keon yelled in defense.

"Nigga, get the hell on, before you end up like him! I don't fuck with you, and you don't fuck with mine, step!" Yaheem said as he got in his face. Keon nodded with a hateful look on his face.

"I ain't have shit to do with this!" Keon hollered as he walked away with his fist balled up as he entered the club.

"Duchess, you good?" Trigga questioned as he patted me on the shoulder.

"I-I think so..." He nodded.

"Here, take her car to the garage. I'll come get it in the morning," Yaheem said, passing him my keys. Trigga nodded as they dapped up and told Yaheem to call him up later. Yaheem nodded and picked me up, carrying me to his car.

"Yah... I'm so sorry. I—"

"Shh, it ain't yo' fault, baby... Let's just get you home. Daddy will take care of you, I got'chu." He kissed my forehead and I nuzzled into his neck as he put me in the car. Trigga got in my car, driving to the garage, as one of his goons followed us to the house. I don't know how I survived this night, but I was glad. It was some things I had to realize about myself, and I had to do better. This couldn't be my life anymore.

Chapter 11

Yaheem

"You know you're not going back to that club, right? I mean that shit, you working there is over," I said to her sternly as I rubbed her feet. She just looked off into space. I knew she was thinking about what had happened to her and I couldn't let her stay in that place. "Ayo! Earth to Duchess?" I said, waving my hand in her face, but she was just so out of it. I rubbed her foot one last time before rubbing my hands together. And, when I slapped her ass while squeezing it, she snapped back.

"Ow! Why you do that?" she screeched, rubbing her ass.

"You was ignoring a nigga, you okay?" I asked, making sure. Duchess batted those beautiful eyes of her.

"Sorry. I was... just thinking, that's all." I pulled her into me.

"Don't let it get to you. I know what happened to you is going to take some time to get over. But I'm here and it'll never happen again." She nodded. "Just chill with me. That dude will never hurt you again. I swear... And I swear, Duchess, you not going back there. I mean it. You don't need that place." She laid her head on my chest.

"I have dreams, I need to get over my problems in my life. I should've been a dancer, not a stripper. I knew what this life would bring, and I got sucked into it. If I could be a dancer like I dreamed, I'd love to do that. And go to college..." she said with a broad smile as she thought on her dreams and ambitions.

"Anything you dream, you can do it. You got a second chance, and you can do it," I said. Duchess smiled and pecked my cheek. Her phone began to buzz. Duchess let out a deep breath before she pointed for me to hand her the phone.

Reaching over to the bedside table and grabbing the phone. I glanced at the caller ID, and it was one of the twins.

"It's yo girl, Leiloni. You want to answer it and talk to her right now? Or wait?" I asked Duchess. She nodded, so I passed her the phone as she looked at all the texts. The phone stopped ringing.

"Let me call her back." I nodded while Duchess snuggled against me. I heard the phone ringing as she pressed it to her ear.

"Hello. Yeah, I'm fine, I just had to leave the club early, after that fight with Candice. I'm home now, but I won't be coming back. No, you don't have to tell Miss Coffee, I'll let him know myself," Duchess said on the phone. I made sure no one at the club knew what happened to her. I didn't need anyone making her situation worse. I was gone handle that shit myself.

"Bitch, who was there? No fucking way are you serious? Well duh, if I was there, I would have even been discovered too! you gotta be kidding me. So, who did she scout out?" She smacked her lips as she got off of me. Looking her way, I raised my eyebrow. "I can't deal..."

"What's up?" I asked. She held up her finger, signaling me, *one minute*.

"Man, alright. I gotta go. I'll hit y'all back later." And with that, Duchess hung up the phone and tossed the phone on the bed.

What's up, ma?" I asked again as I grabbed her shoulders.

"Man, those bitches lucked up tonight! Fuck, I can't catch a break!" Duchess yelled.

"You gone tell me what happened though? Come on," I said kissing her shoulder.

"Fucking Cardi B. and the Migos was there! They got most of the strippers to be in they video, like what the fuck! I could've got that spot. That shit would've opened doors for me!"

"Man, ma, you gone be good. Trust me, don't let that shit get to you! Listen, I know people, got funds, and more shit. I can get you the life you always wanted, Duchess, just believe me. Baby, I got you." Leaning her back on me, I kissed the top of her head as I rubbed her arms. She finally relaxed into me, "You good? You feel better?" She looked up and gave me a sad face.

"No. Gimme kiss." Duchess asked me as she looked up towards me, pursing her lips as she grabbed the side of my face as the kiss deepened. Kissing her lips again, I turned her around and sat her in my lap. "Mmm, give me another kiss," she said, looking in my eyes as I rubbed her back. Pulling Duchess close to me, I tongue kissed her as I grabbed her neck softly.

Through every kiss, I made sure to complement her. Then she said, "We not about to be friends," she said through kisses.

"Flip flop ass." I deepened the kiss just a little bit before she pulled away to get up and pulled off her big sweatshirt letting it fall to the floor.

"I'm going to take a bath," she said, blowing me a kiss.

"Man, you something else, I swear..." I said, licking my lips and was 'bout to get up.

"No, you stay there. I just need some me-time, okay? Just need to get my head right," Duchess said as she switched away into the master bathroom.

"Well, I could've made the bath water for you, but I'll go get you some candles and shit. So don't get in there yet. Just lay here in the bed naked and relax. You don't gotta do nothing," I said, while getting up and walking it the bathroom.

Grabbing her softly and pulling her into my arms, I kissed her again. "Thank you. But you don't gotta do all that," she said while blushing.

"Yes, I do, now do what daddy says and go lay down. It won't take me long," I said to Duchess as I kissed her one more time, before letting her walk back into the room. I was going to enjoy her company. This is all I wanted.

***

Trigga

I just looked at Keon as he downed beer after beer. This nigga was wilding out for nothing, he was acting off lately, and it was making me look at him sideways about what happened to Duchess earlier. "The hell is wrong with you, mane?" I questioned. He was popping X and spazzing out, shit was weird.

"Nothing dawg, man, I just don't. I just can't believe he'd blame me for that shit... Swear to God, I didn't set Duchess up," Keon said, but deep inside, I didn't believe him. He was about to drink another beer, but I snatched it away. He was sloppy drunk, couldn't control his liquor, and we didn't need no bullshit popping off.

A girl came up to Keon. "What's up, sexy, you should buy me a drink," she said with a wink. Then out of nowhere, he began to feel and touch up on her. The reason why Duchess wasn't trying to get back with him. Keon couldn't keep his hands to himself for shit.

"Mmm, daddy, you tryna' roll out with me?" She said licking on his ear. He gone say yes.

"Fasho', mami." I shook my head.

"I'm finna slide out. Exactly why you don't got Duchess, look how you act, nigga," I said, loud enough for him to hear it.

"Nigga what?" he snapped. "Say that again?"

"Take yo' drunk ass on, Keon. Yo' ass trippin. I'm out." I paid for my shit and made my way out. It was time for Yaheem to know some shit. Keon was being real finicky tonight, not his usual self. Now after tonight, the realization set in that he did have something to do what *with* happened to Duchess. Shit was just off. He picked a night where Yaheem would be either coming to the club late, or not coming at all. That made me wonder why she was leaving the club late. This was just fucked up. He knew exactly where she was, at the right time. Too strange. Keon is messing with the wrong peeps and Yaheem is one of them.

Monet Dragun

Chapter 12

Duchess

It was 3:30 a.m. and I still couldn't sleep. Shit was crazy, Yaheem over here growling like a bear makes it even worse. I tried so hard to turn over and ignore it, but it wasn't working. "Ugh! I wish you'd hush! Damn!" I slid out of the bed and grabbed my pillow. I went downstairs and laid on the puffy, soft sofa of his. I could've picked one of his guest bedrooms, but his couch and huge TV would be better.

"Dammit. I forgot my blanket." I sighed to myself and got up from the couch before I could turn the TV on. But I tripped over something on the floor. "The hell?" I fumbled and picked up whatever it was as I flicked on the light. It was a big bag and I unzipped it just to see money and drugs. Shaking my head and sighing, I zipped it back and slid it back under the couch. I didn't want Yaheem to think I was going through his things. I pushed my hair back as I trucked back up the stairs. Going back into his room, this nigga was the weirdest sleeper ever, but yet he was so fine. I got a blanket off the bed. Besides, he didn't care to sleep under the covers anyway. He got the sheet, he'll be cool.

"Voshon? Don't go that way. D-don't leave..." I heard him say lowly in his sleep. I looked over and he was still knocked out. *Who is Voshon?*

I looked at him closely as he started to shift and twist. "Voshon... Don't die on me!" He screamed an earth-shattering scream, grabbed something from under his pillow and aimed it at me. "Who the fuck there!" I ducked down as he pointed the gun at me while he dripped in sweat.

"Oh, shit! Yaheem! It's me, oh my God! It's me! Put the gun down!" My hands shot up as it took him a minute, but he slowly put the gun down. "Are you okay?" I said, holding my hand against my heart, standing up straight and looking at him crazy as I backed up against the wall.

"I-I'm fine..." Yaheem said looking down at the gun he had just put down and laid on his back.

"You sure? Cause you was just mumbling something in your sleep, then sat up screaming and tried to shoot me!" I screamed.

"I'm sorry. Duchess, I just lost my head, it-it was just a nightmare," he said, not even looking my way.

"Okay, but who is Voshon? Do you want to talk about it?" I asked Yaheem again.

"No. Just come get back in bed. And lay next to me. I'ma be cool," he said dryly.

"Okay, grouchy. I'ma just go back downstairs. I'm going to go sleep on the couch. I'm not about to lay in that bed. You might try and choke me in my sleep." He leaned up and cut his eyes at me.

"Man, come get in the bed... I want you next to me," he said as we stared at each other.

"Uh-uh, I haven't gotten any sleep whatsoever. Go to sleep, good night. I'm goin' downstairs." He scoffed and laid back down. That was the craziest thing I'd ever seen. I made my way down the steps and dived on the couch. It was pitch black and quiet in the house. My eyes closed as I finally fell into a deep slumber.

***

Yaheem

Waking up the next morning, I was tired as hell. That nightmare I had last night was wild. I haven't had one of those since I was eighteen years old, when he had got murdered. Why was they coming back now? No time for me to be feeling weak, I had to get it together quick.

I didn't mean to jump up pointing a gun at my girl. But, in that dream I thought I'd seen my brother's killer, it was so blurry, but I could've sworn I saw who it was. Now she think I'm crazy as fuck. Getting out the bed fast, I immediately felt the room spin. "Shit..." I said, trying to regain my vision. I rubbed my eyes and sat down, trying to relax. It was something going on with me and I had to figure it out.

"Damn," I said, once I felt myself getting back to normal. I got up slowly and moved slowly out of the bedroom. The smell of food cooking hit my nose. Smiling, I went into the bathroom to take care of myself.

After, I did my hygiene shit, I went downstairs to where Duchess was. "Morning beautiful, how you doing?" I said while grabbing her, wrapping my arms around her waist.

"Morning. I'm good, but the question is how you feeling, daddy?" She pecked my cheek as she put the last pancake on the plate.

"This looks good... And smells good too," I said as I picked up a sausage link.

"Thanks. That's your plate, you can eat," she said with a warm smile as she sat down at the counter and blessed the food.

She really didn't look my way, just looked at her phone as she ate. "So, I'm sorry bout last night, I didn't know how to come to you this morning," I said, trying to get her to look at me. She shrugged.

"It's fine, I guess..." She kept eating her food while she continued to look at something on her phone.

"It is not fine, Duchess. I shouldn't have did that. It's just, I'm still fighting demons and some stuff I just don't want to talk about... right now," I stated.

"That's okay, Yaheem." Duchess finally looked at me. She rubbed my hand, but then pinched me.

"Ow! What was that for!?" I said, rubbing my arm.

"For pointing that gun at me, nigga!" she said, rolling her eyes. So, I rolled my eyes back.

"I said sorry, damn... sharp ass nails, I'ma cut them shits off. Do it again," I said as while getting back to eating my food. Then out of nowhere, she pinched me again and I cut my eyes at her. I shot up from the chair at the counter and held her tight as I bit in her neck.

"Ah! Stop, you vampire!" She giggled.

"Pinch me again and see me doing that again." I chuckled as I smacked her ass. "Why is it so big?" I said, biting my lip.

"Stop it, don't start! Finish eating, Yaheem."

I cracked a smile and started eating again. My phone rang and I looked down at it. Trigga was calling me, it was too early to be hitting the traps. But it could be anything else, taking a big gulp of OJ, I answered the phone.

"What's the word?" I said, clearing my throat as I ate.

"Aye mane, I gotta tell you some shit, like real talk. Meet me at Buckley and 49th Street." I raised my eyebrow cause this was not like my homie, I knew it was some shit. Duchess finished her plate and got up as she kissed my cheek.

"Uh, okay bro, I'll be there," I replied. Trigga said some other stuff and I nodded. I looked up to Duchess putting her plate in the sink and cleaning up the kitchen. This is something I'd love to see every day, her sexy ass moving around my crib. I just stared at that ass. After she did that, she walked over to me, wrapping her arms around my neck, kissing and biting on me.

"Y-yeah man, I feel you... I'll be there in five." I hung up and kissed Duchess. "You a nasty girl, I swear." She giggled and pecked my lips, before she went to go sit on the couch and watch *The Game* on *Paramount+*.

"I gotta be somewhere. So, you got the big house to yourself till I get back. You gone be cool?" She pouted.

"Okay. And yeah, I'ma be cool..." I kissed her lip as I took her bottom lip in my mouth.

"Stop all that pouting, I'ma be back. If you need anything, text me. But I stocked up the fridge and shit too, so no need for you to leave the crib if you don't want to." She smiled as I turned around and she grabbed my booty. And stuck her tongue out at me.

"Don't do that shit Duchess..." She busted out laughing and I shook my head as I went upstairs. I kept wondering what Trigga gotta tell me. The shit had me thinking if it had something to do with what happened to Duchess.

Monet Dragun

Chapter 13

Duchess

I just couldn't stay in this big ass house by myself. Yaheem was so sweet to stop by my house the other day and bring me a bag of clothes. He even bought me some new shit, which he didn't have to do but still, he did. Putting on my black, velour two-piece jogging suit, with my off-white and black Jordan's. Then I slid on some 90s girl style hoops, and I didn't feel like putting on my contacts, so I just put on my thick rim glasses. I let my long, naturally bone-straight hair down as I checked my outfit in the mirror. The crop top jacket showed off my belly button and tiny heart tattoo.

I had to take out them damn weave clip in pieces. Had my head itching. If my brother seen me with that in my head, he'd crack jokes at me. Just thinking about him, I missed Reese so much, hadn't heard from him in so long. I know he was living his life, but it was like he had forgotten all about me. So, I shot him a text, hoping he'd respond back.

Sighing, I slid my phone into my purse. Checking my lip gloss in the mirror, I was good to go. I didn't put on any make-up, I didn't need it. Today was my last and final day at Diamond City. It was time to go on to bigger and better things. I locked up Yaheem's house and got in my Hellcat. I Blue-toothed my phone as I started it up and played my bad bitch playlist, the first song that came on was by Saweetie. Backing out, I drove off to Diamond City.

Her song blasted through my car speakers as I sang along to the lyrics. The drive there was peaceful. I was going to do better in life, maybe become a real respectable dancer or something more, who knows. No less than thirty minutes later, I pulled up to the place and cut off my car. I had a new and bright future, but first this has to end before I can start anew. A car pulling up made me look to see who it was, Bubbles hopped out and immediately looked at me. The look on his face said it all. "Yo' Duch, c'mere, man. You good? I swear, if I was there that night, I would've beat him to a bloody pulp." Walking over to him, he hugged me.

"Yeah, I know, Bubbles. I know you would have. But trust me, I'm good now, for real." Pulling away from the hug, he nodded, he knew why I was here.

"Yeah, it's too early for you to be here, shorty. So, you finally leaving, huh?" he asked me.

"Yep, this life just isn't for me anymore. Done with it all," I said to Bubbles. He smiled as he dapped me up.

"Yeah, you def better than this place. Go live your life," he said. I nodded and said my goodbyes before I walked away and to the club entrance. Walked in with my head held high like I always would. Blu, like always, stared a damn hole in my neck as I walked in. Her face was still bruised up from the beatdown I gave her a couple days ago.

"Make-up will fix that right up, honey... You should use me," I said, laughing my way away from her. She scowled at me, and I turned on my heels, going to the boss' office.

I knocked on his door and heard moaning from inside, but ain't no way Miss Coffee was getting dick in the club. Thought he was better than that shit. I just slipped my resignation papers under the door. I don't even have time for the bullshit. Pushing my hair back and walking out of this sorry ass place, I heard someone call my name out of nowhere. *Keon.*

"What?" I said with attitude and was very uninterested in what he had to say.

He held up his hands in defense. "I just want to talk, that's all..." he said. Looking him up and down, I wondered why the fuck was he here.

"The fuck are you doing here, bro?" I questioned as I snatched away from him.

"I came to see if you was here, just to talk. That's all, Duchess. I need to fix this... us," he pleaded. Sighing, I was just about to give him some of my time. Before my ex-best friend that he cheated on me with, walked up beside him and started kissing on him.

"Duchess, it's not what it looks like," Keon pleaded.

Waving my hand in his face while laughing, I said, "I don't give a fuck what it looks like. We have nothing to talk about. Talk to that bitch, cause it's obvious yo ass haven't changed..." He was about to say something before I put my hand up, signaling him to just stop talking. Leaving out the club, Keon was following behind me, still pleading his case. I ignored it. Getting in my car and starting it up, I pulled off, giving they asses both the middle finger. I'm way better than this shit...

***

Trigga

We sat on the porch of my auntie's crib just like we did back in the day. Yaheem was sipping on Henny and eating some of my auntie's ribs. I was doing the same as I explained everything to Yaheem. Surprisingly, he was keeping his composure.

"So, what you're trying to tell me is..." he paused as he finished his last rib. "That he been plotting ways to get her back for the longest?" he questioned.

"Yeah, Keon is cool, but he got a deep wicked mind for real... I just fear he may be on the breaking point to doing something stupid." He nodded, wiping his hands off as he sat there, processing everything I just told him and ran his hand through his dreads.

"Mane, thanks for the info and I'ma need to know more about his past..." Yaheem said.

"This water runs deep, Yaheem, mane. You know he was fucking with Keyonna heavy. Before he met Duchess and before she started working at the club? Then soon after, he started talking to Duchess. You don't remember when Keyonna just up and disappeared?"

"Nah, I don't remember. I really didn't fuck with him like that..." he said, eyeing me while trailing off his sentence.

"I'ma refresh yo' memory, bro. She used to switch yo' Glock with a Nerf Gun, and fuck with yo' ass. Keyonna, man," I said to him, then as it clicked for Yaheem, he looked at me with his eyes wide.

"Yo' baby sister, Keyonna, Lil Key Key!" Yaheem said.

"Yeah man, the day she up and vanished is the day she spent a day with him. He was so-called spoiling her. My baby sister didn't tell me much, she wanted to be treated grown and not babied by me. So, she stayed at his crib, and I haven't seen her since. He had an alibi, but I believe otherwise. I don't think he kilt her. I *know* he did, man. My sister loved his ass, all he did was cheat and lie, and she was too naïve to believe it, or believe me when I was telling her right.

"Keon didn't want Keyonna to leave him, and she was that day. I know he had something to do with it." He looked at me like I lost my mind. "Believe me, man. One of his screws is loose as fuck. Keep him the fuck away from Duchess. I put that on everything. I ain't lying. And we boys, you should know my word is bond." Yaheem nervously nodded and got up to go to his car.

"I'ma believe you, man... But this shit really creeped out a nigga. Why didn't you tell me this before? We supposed to be boys," Yaheem said.

"Tell me about it. But shid, it was something I was dealing with. That's something we don't discuss in our parts, you know that. Once they gone, they gone. But I really miss her, man," I said, rubbing my hand down my face.

"You right. All that is true, and I know the feeling, dawg," Yaheem said as he got in his whip. Yaheem needs to find out everything. There's things I've been trying to connect for years and now they're falling into place. But I know Keon ain't in his right head. Especially when it comes to females. He just can't take no for an answer. I wish I'd seen that when my sister was alive. He wouldn't be going nowhere near her. It's something about him when it comes to females. And I know my sister learned the hard way.

Yaheem, got in his car and pulled off with worry written all over his face. I just pray Duchess isn't Keon's next victim...

Chapter 14

Keon

It was something about Duchess, I just couldn't live without her. We had something special before I got caught fucking her friend. That was never supposed to happen. I wanted to cut it off with that bitch, but her pussy was just too good. The fact that I had two bad bitches was me having my cake and eating it too. I had commitment problems, but that didn't mean I didn't love the fuck outta Duchess. Her bitch ass friend was the reason we got caught in the first place.

Duchess didn't want shit to do with me, and I never had a female not come back to me. But I have had a bitch make me lose my self-control, and I wasn't going back to that man I used to be. The way I want Duchess, I just need her back in my life. If I can't have her, she won't have Yaheem either and that was something I meant.

"Nigga, you look like a damn crack head, sit down. The fuck," Trigga said, rolling his eyes at me.

"Man, shut up! I lost every chance of getting her back! Nigga, you don't understand!" I was antsy and shaking.

"Nigga, you need to chill! Fuck wrong with'cha?" he said, looking at me sideways. I just sat down and stared at my feet, not listening to anything coming out of his mouth. I was mastering my next plan on getting back with Duchess, "Keon?" he said, shaking me.

He snapped his fingers in my face, making me look up at him. "Yeah?" I looked at him and Trigga looked at me strangely.

"You good, man?"

"I'm fine, bro, for real," was all I said. Trigga nodded and turned away from me as he looked at his phone. I didn't pay him any attention. I was coming up with a plan... And it was going to work. I just had to get her mind off that nigga, she was good at trusting anyway, so I knew that wasn't going to be hard. I needed to be quick about this, so I made some calls. She wasn't going to slip from me again.

"Yo, you being weird, dude. Where the bricks at, so I can be on my fucking way, I got other shit to handle and money to make. Nigga, if you ain't gone do that, then I'm out," Trigga said as he stood up from the chair. Waving my hand at him, I threw him the bag.

"Man, I don't need the shit today, but get that shit to that nigga, bro. Fuck, I need a friend and you worried about this shit." Trigga grabbed the bag as he still chewed on the toothpick from earlier. Taking the toothpick out, he looked me square in the face and said, "Listen bruh, we ain't friends, alright? Let's get that shit straight, for real. Yo ass over here tripping over a bitch that ain't yours and you'll never have again. Now my boy, he in that shit, move on. That's yo problem right there, you worried about bitches more than money."

"Man... get the fuck out my crib, dawg, talking all that shit! I don't give a fuck about these bitches, they just pussy to me, nigga," I said to Trigga with venom in my tone.

"So, my sister Keyonna was just pussy, huh nigga? You said you loved my sister and would go to war to find out who killed her. What happened to that, huh? What happened to that! Now you chasing after another girl, just like you did Key Key? Bitch, fuck you!" Trigga yelled as he looked me up and down. I had no words left to say after that.

"That's what I thought, you know what I'm about. Sorry ass nigga." He walked out and slammed the door behind him. I had put what happened to Keyonna in the furthest part of my mind, but him bringing it up only made my blood boil. Women who didn't control their mouths around me made me rage to the point where I couldn't control myself. But I changed... I was a different man now, wasn't I?

***

Duchess

It was weeks later, and I felt new and refreshed. No toxic bitches in my face, no grimy men trying to holla at me, and no dusty job to keep me broken at night. I had a dude that cared for me like no one had before. But my guard was still up and taking it slow was the only way to go right now. Yaheem was so fine, the way he looked in the kitchen cooking for me with no shirt on made my body tingle. Looking at him while I bit my lip, "Mmm, Yaheem you look so damn scrumptious," I said to him, biting my finger as he turned back and looked at me with a smirk.

"I do, huh, well get used to this. You'll see this every day," Yaheem said smiling at me. I laughed and smiled back as my phone rang. Turning to where it was, I pulled it off the charger and looked at who was calling me. My eyes lit up as I saw it was my brother.

"Yaheem, be quiet, okay? This my brother." He looked at me sideways as I answered the phone. "Oh my God! Reese! I miss you so much. I'm sorry for causing that scene before you left," I whined into the phone.

"Sis, I was acting like an ass too. I'm sorry for the way I acted. And I know, Sis, I miss you too. I'll be home soon." I was overwhelmed with excitement, it felt like forever since he left. Before I could say something, Yaheem yelled from the kitchen.

"Aye, bae, what you want to eat?" Yaheem loud ass said. I knew my brother was going to say something now.

"Who in the hell is that calling you bae, Duchess Brie?" Tyreese said loudly into the phone. I bit the corner of my lip and thought of what to say next.

"Uh, well… big brother, I am grown, okay? But that's my boyfriend and—"

"*Boyfriend,* aw hell naw! You wait till I leave to get a boyfriend. *Again*! The last nigga you was with I didn't like, Duchess! So, what about this one, he a hustla too?" He shouted into the phone, I had to take that shit from my damn ear. Yaheem looked like he was under gun point by the stare I was giving him.

"Thanks so much!" I semi-whispered. He put his hands up and I gave him a stank face. Now I must put up with my brother.

"Well, yeah. But his occupation has nothing to do with us dating. He's a good guy, Reese! Stop being so overprotective, okay?" I said, biting my nails before Yaheem swatted my hand away.

"Man, fuck that. Nice my ass, what he do for a living and don't you lie to me. Your wellbeing is all I care about, if that nigga bringing shit around you. You never know what can happen." Shit, shit, *SHIT*!

"Reese, come on with that. Why do you have to act like this?" I said, growing annoyed at this point.

"So, you not gone tell me then? Is he a hustla?" Reese said louder into the phone.

"Yes, he is. What's the big deal?"

"Really! I know you like the back of my damn hand. You didn't learn your lesson from Keon's punk ass? These thugs just use and abuse women, look what happened to Momma!" I sighed and that was enough conformation for him.

"Reese, he is different. And I'm not going to end up like Mom. So don't even bring her and that situation up to me, for real, Reese." I sighed.

"Man, you know what? I called to check on you and patch things up with you, Duchess. I'ma talk to you later before you raise my damn blood pressure... I love you. But you better be careful, I mean it. Don't get caught up in no bullshit." I nodded as if he could see me.

"I will. But you gotta stop treating me like a baby." I mentally kicked myself for not telling my brother what happened with Marco. And I didn't want the word to get to him before I told him.

"Yeah... alright, bye. And tell that nigga *Yaheem* I'm that nigga and he bet not fuck up. He better be good to you. I got eyes everywhere." I rolled my eyes. But he wasn't lying.

"Okay, Reese, I love you too..." I whined. He skipped over my baby act and got off the phone with an attitude. When I put my phone down, I turned my attention to Yaheem. He was eating a candy bar while turning on his PS5 with his controller. I gave him a cute smile then punched the shit outta him.

"The hell, girl! Ow, that shit hurt, what is wrong with you?" he said, popping me back softly.

"You gotta big mouth! I told you don't say a word while I was on the phone with my brother. Now he grilling me," I said while pushing my hair back. Yaheem looked at me with a pouty face. "Mm-hmm. I needed to tell him on my own time. No, I'm not hiding you, he's just overprotective."

"Aye, I'm sorry, but don't be hittin' me, girl." I huffed and popped him again. This time on the side of the head. He glared at me, and we started play fighting.

"Get yo' big ass off me, you are too heavy, Yaheem..." I giggled as he tried to pin me down.

"Then you give up. Say you give up and stop hitting me." I bit his hand and took advantage.

"I don't play fair." I smirked as we flipped over and I pinned him down, then stuck my tongue out at him.

"Me either." He got his hand free and slapped the fuck out of my ass. "Now get yo' heavy fat ass off me," he said giving me a goofy face.

"You love this fat ass though," I said, jiggling it on him.

"Maybe." He smirked, smacking it again. We paused and just stared at each other. He was so sexy, the way his jaw flexed when he looked at me. His eyes glimmered while I looked into them, it was like his eyes was tied to something special. The way I wanted to find out more about him was crazy. His full lips were so plump and juicy as he licked them, and his grillz just made his facial features so damn fine.

It was like we were stuck in time. I couldn't find words to say to him, but I was feeling something. "Yaheem?"

"Yeah, ma?" he said, looking back at me, his looks just made me melt. And at that moment, I caught myself as my mouth became dry, and all my words were lost in my throat. "Wassup?"

"Oh, um… never mind, it's nothing," I said with a smile. He raised his eyebrow but shrugged it off as he put his attention back on the game. Was I falling in love with him? If I was to say it, would he say it back? My mind was just running as he was sitting there playing *2K* and oblivious to my thoughts. I began overthinking and biting my fresh new set of nails. Catching myself, I just went for it. "I love you…" I blurted out. His head turned around in slow motion.

"You what?" he questioned. I rolled my eyes.

"You heard me, Yaheem."

"No, say it again." I sighed and swallowed hard. "I said, I love you, Yaheem." I couldn't read his face and he just nodded. No words were said between the two of us for a minute. "Say something," I said.

He looked back at me as he opened his mouth to speak. I was looking for those words to slip outta his mouth, but they didn't. "I don't know if I can say that just yet, Duchess," he said, rubbing the back of his neck. I automatically felt dumb. And at that moment I was stuck thinking, why did I say that stupid shit in the first place.

"Duchess, talk to me," he said, grabbing my chin softly.

"Uh, yeah... I understand," I said, brushing it off and pushing his hand away. Getting up from the couch, trying not to show my real feelings.

"Duchess, listen, it's not like that. I swear, it's just—"

"You don't have to explain why, Yaheem. For real," I said, turning back around and walking out of the living room and leaving him to sit there by himself on the couch. That was one thing I should have never let slip out. And I'll never do it again.

Chapter 15

Yaheem

It took me a minute for me to get up from the couch because I was stunned. But I couldn't just sit here and ignore her feelings. The way she looked at me, I knew she was hurt by what I had said. I made her feel so dumb for saying, "I love you" and me not saying it back. It was hard for me to say that shit. It's not like I don't feel the same way. I do, but it's hard for a nigga to put his feelings out there. I'd been here once before, and it didn't go well.

Duchess was different and she was special to me. Not saying she's like every other woman. But ol' girl I was fucking with back then, my head was gone for that bitch, that I was the shorty I was going to marry. But she rejected me, pretty much used me for my money. I know Duchess was not like that, but it's hard.

I can't bring myself to say "I love you" again, not right now. I rubbed my hair, kind of scared to look her in those beautiful eyes. I pulled my shirt over my head as I walked out of the living room and went to see where she was. Checking every room, I finally found her in her favorite room, filled with fluffy beanbags and a swing bed. She was on her laptop doing something, but when I came in, she didn't look my way.

"Duchess?" I said as she finally looked up.

"Huh?" she questioned.

"I'm sorry for real, man. Just shit run deeper than what you—" She held up her hand for me to stop talking.

"I said, you ain't have to explain. It's fine, Yaheem," she said coldly.

"But it's not fine. I'm trying to tell you something," I said, getting closer to her.

"What? A sad storyline? I really don't want to hear it, okay? I've heard it before, okay Yaheem? Now I'm trying to sign up for these classes." She directed her attention back to her laptop.

"Man, fuck! Just listen, damn! I'm trying to get some shit off my chest, and you won't even hear me out?" She shrugged. "That's bullshit, man. Real talk, fuck this shit."

"Whatever, I'm going back to my crib today anyway," Duchess said. I didn't have time for this. Walking out of the room, I fanned her off. Making my way back into the bedroom, I put on my hat and slipped on my Nike sandals, before I trucked out the front door. Slamming it on my way out. She being real petty for nothing. I was trying to tell her the truth.

***

Keon

"Round two," I said to myself, bracing myself as I rang her doorbell for her to buzz me in. Waiting for her to come to the door, hopefully.

"What?" she shouted out of her window.

"Can we talk, shorty? Please?" She rolled her eyes and shut her window. Groaning, I began to turn around. When I got halfway down the path, her front door opened. She was dressed in a big t-shirt and spandex shorts matched with teddy slippers. Her hair was dressed in a messy bun as she wore her glasses. Duchess was just so fine that it was a damn shame.

"What is it you wanna talk about? Cause I don't have time for this today. Choose what you gotta say wisely." I smiled and walked back towards her apartment.

"I'm not on no bullshit, I swear," I said to her. Duchess nodded and made a path for me to come inside. She let me in then shut the door. Mr. Steal Ya' Girl is in effect. The house smelled like her favorite incense.

"Can I take my shoes off? You gotta nice place, Duchess," I said, trying to make some kind of conversation.

"Yeah, sit on the sofa. I'm making my tea. What you gotta talk about?" Duchess asked, getting straight to the point.

"Come on, I'm trying to take you out for lunch and get back in your good graces, for real. I know what I did was wrong, and I hurt you. I just want to fix us."

"First of all, I was never hurt over you. You just fucked up what I had. So, if you wanna take me out for the free, I'm down," she said with a shrug. "You keep asking, so might as well." She finished making her tea and walked into her living room as she began to talk to me. I had one chance to make shit happen, and this was my chance.

***

Brent Faiyaz blasted in the club as I walked in. Duchess agreed to go out with me, just as friends. But she didn't know Yaheem would be there. I had all this shit set the fuck up. "Drink?"

"Nah, I'm fine," she said as she rubbed her arm.

"Relax, I'm not going to bite," I said playfully. She gave me a half smile.

"I'll just take a Coke. That's all, no liquor." I nodded. I got up and looked across the room where Yaheem was. I smirked and got her drink when he looked like he saw someone. Perfect. I called over the waiter and waited for him to swing by us.

"So, why did you cheat? What's the point of trying to get back with me if you cheated?" Duchess asked as we got our drinks.

"I don't know, it wasn't you or your fault. I was dumb to do that shit and cheat on you. Dumbest thing I could've did was to lose you, ma. I regret that shit every day and seeing you with that nigga just made me want to show you I'm better than what I was." Before she could respond to what I had said, Yaheem came out of nowhere yelling.

"Duchess?" I heard Yaheem shout. I made it back to the table and he looked at me crazy. "Fuck you with him for? The fuck is going on?" he said in a mad tone, looking as if he was about to explode.

"Calm down, Yaheem, damn. It's not that serious, okay?" she said, crossing her arms and rolling her eyes.

"So, this what we do now?" She shrugged.

"Alright then. Remember that shit, I'm dead ass, Duchess." He walked past me, and I bumped his shoulder. "Better watch who you touching, dude."

"*Baby,* just sit down," Duchess said. Yaheem gave her the evilest glare ever.

"You tripping, real talk. All this cause I didn't say I love you back? You really acting like a hoe right now! I'm out," he yelled. Her mouth dropped wide open.

"Who you calling a hoe!" Duchess said, grabbing his arm. Yaheem snatched from her.

"Man, fuck you! Remember, *he* yo' baby. I'm out this bitch. Keon, I'ma see yo punk ass, bitch. Believe that, nigga." He fixed his cap and walked out of the club. I just stood there looking as innocent as possible. Plan complete...

Chapter 16

Duchess

I just looked at him as he made his way out of this place. What I did was too far and now my feelings were really all over the place. I ran my hands through my hair feeling really embarrassed. The talk me and Keon had, we agreed just to be friends. I had deep feelings for Yaheem but this shit confusing me. Making Yaheem jealous was to only make him realize how much he loved me. But I was looking stupid right now, I never wanted to chase him away.

"You good?" I looked past Keon. To be smart, I really do some stupid ass shit.

"Can we just go? I don't wanna be here anymore."

"But we just got here. You gone make that nigga change our plans? Food not even here yet," he said, looking up at me.

"I just wanna go home. I don't even care anymore. Maybe another time, Keon. That was just too much," I said, looking down. He nodded and I got up, making my way towards the exit with Keon right behind me.

"Aye, bitch! You should stop being a hoe!" I heard a familiar female voice call out. I snapped my head and looked around to notice Blu dying of laughter with a drink in her hand, while she sat on some nigga's lap. I chuckled and walked over towards her.

"Just leave well enough alone, Duchess, she ain't worth it," I heard Keon say, but I have a short temper and I'm sick of her loudmouth ass. I slapped the drink out of her hand and slapped the shit out of her. Sent her flying right out of the man's lap. He put his hands up in surrender as I continued to whoop her ass.

"Always talking that shit, bitch, but can't never throw them hands!" I felt someone tug on my waist, sending me kicking and swinging. Keon was dragging me out of the club. "Put me down, dammit!"

"Not until you calm the fuck down. Pouncing on her like a little ass squirrel," he said chuckling, but I didn't find it funny whatsoever. I shoved him away from me as I walked to his car. "Aye, calm all that down, ma."

"I'm not your *ma*, I have a name. Fuck!" I said as he opened the door for me and I got inside, plopping down in the seat and slamming the door.

"Duchess, don't be slamming my damn door. You break it, you buy it."

"Shut the fuck up," I said, closing my arms over my chest. Not even realizing that my boobs were popping out, I looked over at him as he was drooling like a damn puppy. "Creep." I fixed my dress and he chuckled as he started up the car and pulled off. His hand crept up to my thigh and I swatted it away.

"No touching. If we gone be friends, there are rules. I'm not even joking with you."

"But you called me baby," he said smirking.

"Keon, the fuck. That do not mean anything. I told you, it was only to make him jealous. Now I may have lost him, because of this damn game I'm playing," I said, looking out the window.

"Well, maybe he's not for you." I was about to say something smart as he stopped at the red light.

"Keon, please shut—" he smashed his lips into mine and I found myself trying to push him away, but he held me in place. This wasn't right. My eyes stayed open as I pushed Keon away and slapped him.

"Ow!" he said, rubbing his cheek. "Damn girl, the fuck was that for?" He pulled off.

"Are you dumb? I don't want you like that! I said no touching! Got it?" He shrugged and kept his eyes on the road.

"You liked it though."

"No, I didn't. Don't do that shit again. Fuck off," I said bitterly as I wiped my lips off. "I don't know where the hell yo' lips been."

"They can be on that pussy. You know that shit. You know how my mouth do."

"I know how it talks shit, and how it fills you with playa' lines," I said, biting my nails.

"Can't we just let that go, baby?" he said like a baby.

"I'm not your baby, Keon... like I said, fuck off."

"We can fuck if you like," he said, biting his lip and looking at me. I rolled my eyes and looked the other way. He was getting on my nerves.

"Just shut up." I looked out the window as we cruised down the street. He was doing too much for my comfort, but I just wanted to go home. I was so over tonight, and the bullshit I caused. Soon after the drive, he pulled up to my crib. I quickly exited his car as he was talking. Walking up the path, I heard him behind me and I rolled my eyes.

"What, Keon?" I asked him as he rolled up on me, licking his lips. "Please stop, you're doing too much, okay?"

"Can I come in?" he asked as he stood in the doorway.

"No, not after the stunt you pulled. And I followed suit like a goofy. Just go home," I said, biting my nails and looking at my feet. He moved my hand and looked me in the eyes.

"I can do whatever you like. Fuck the shit out of you, come on. You know how this dick used to make you cum repeatedly.

"No, you can't fuck me. We'll never fuck again. You can't do what he can, okay? We're better off friends. Good-night, Keon." I was about to close the door until he grabbed my hips.

"I can do you better, Duchess." He pulled me to him and kissed me. Sticking his tongue into my mouth, he grabbed my neck and turned his head as his tongue changed directions. But I wasn't into this shit, it wasn't cutting it for me, he wasn't Yaheem.

"Man, why are you acting like this, bro? You're being weird, bye. I'll talk to you whenever, you doing too much." I quickly closed the door and put my back against the door. Keon was doing shit he never did, which was just weird. My phone started to buzz, and it was a text from Yaheem. My heart thumped, but me being dumb, I smacked my lips.

"We need to talk."

But me being stubborn, I relied back, *"Thought I was a hoe..."* I closed my phone and walked down the hall to my room. I sat on my bed and took off my heels as I flopped on the bed. All this was a big mistake. My phone rang and rang, but I didn't answer it. I just wanted to lay here, but my phone chiming was annoying, I shot up from the bed and snatched my phone.

The fuck is she calling me for? "Hello?"

"So, you don't know who your mom is no more?"

***

Yaheem

This shit was blowing me, people go through shit in their relationship every day. But the petty game she was playing and doing little slick shit just to tick me off? I never dealt with any of this in a relationship. I wasn't there with a girl, all I was

134

thinking of was Duchess, to be out with another bitch wasn't me at all. I was there with my crew, smoking a spliff, trying to wrap my head around the situation. Then I see this crazy nigga with Duchess. She don't know how that man really is out here, moving like a weird ass nigga. I been looking into him but muthafuckas wanna be tight lipped.

Then I see her stroll up with that nigga, Keon. Wanting to beat his ass for what Trigga had told me about what happened to his sister Keyonna, all I could think about was Duchess' safety. But how Duchess and I was moving, it made me instantly go back to when my ex-fiancée cheated on me.

I'd just seen it flash before my eyes. I was never a cheater, and I wasn't about to become one, just because a bitch tried to hurt me. If Duchess wanted to be this way, maybe it was time to move on. I rubbed my forehead as I sat at the table, thinking about all this when I had to be making this money. The last customer came up to me and bought a pack. I stuffed my money in my sock and me and Trigga made our way to my whip.

"Aye man, I'ma stop at Duchess' house." He nodded.

"Ight, it's been a minute since I seen Lemon Head," he said. I sighed and started the car. He looked at me. "What's wrong, my boy?" I wiped my hand down my face.

"Man, shorty wildin', we got into it about that love shit. Don't get me wrong. I want her in my life, but damn, it just something about going full throttle for love that got my head fucked up." He gave me the "oh" face and shook his head. I told him the whole story.

"Man, she trippin', she know you got feelings for her. Me and you both know the love shit can turn cold as fuck. Do she know about what happened?" Trigga asked me as he sparked up.

"Nah, she wouldn't let me explain that's how upset she was. Duchess wouldn't let me say shit. Even if I did, she would have still said, fuck me. I know it," I said, shaking my head.

"Let ha' come around, mane." I nodded and was close to her home.

"Well damn, she live over here? Duchess' living nice as fuck." I shrugged. I just needed to talk to her and clear things up. Duchess was going to hear me the fuck out. But one thing I wasn't going to do was chase Duchess. She knew how a nigga felt about her and she was going to feel me for real this time. I pulled into the parking lot and looked for her car. It must have been in the garage, cause she for sure wasn't answering my text or calls. "So sick of this shit, bro, Duchess better be home." Trigga didn't say a word as I cut the engine and hopped out the whip.

Headed up the pathway it was a female was coming out of the apartment as we approached. She looked us up and down as we walked up. She didn't see we had no key, cause she was staring at us so hard.

Licking her lips, she almost dropped her bags as we walked near her and the door. "You good, ma?" Trigga asked as he caught her bags.

"Yeah, I'm good," she said, looking him up and down one more time. Trigga smiled as his grillz glistened, she was in la-la land. Shaking my head as I grabbed the door and walked in, Trigga said he'd holla at shorty, and he walked in behind me. Jogging up the steps, I got to her floor and knocked on the door. We could slightly hear her playing music, so I knocked a little harder.

"Who is it?" she yelled as I leaned against the door frame.

"Duchess, open the door, shorty," I said, rubbing my forehead.

"And I said, who is it?" Duchess said smartly.

"Man... Duch, it's Yaheem. Now come on, open the door," I said annoyed. The sound of locks unlocking made me sigh as she finally opened the door. Duchess stood there in a satin two-piece set, the top was cropped as it showed off her belly button and hourglass thick figure. Shorty was looking scrumptious, and I wanted to eat her up. But I was pissed at what the fuck she did.

"Yo," she said with her hand on her hip.

"Yo? Man, don't play with me, Duchess." I pushed past and into her crib. I could smell the Bath & Body Works candle she had lit. Trigga walked in, and she locked the front door.

"What do you want, Yaheem? And hey, Tyson," she said to Trigga. Now how the hell she know his *real* name?

"How you know Trigga?" I questioned.

"Used to be cool with his sister, we went to school together. But like I said, what you want, Yaheem?" she said with attitude. Grabbing her elbow, I pulled her closer to me.

"Man, watch yo mouth, in the bedroom now," I said.

Trigga sat on her couch and shouted to her, "Aye girl, stop callin' me by my government, you know I got warrants," turning on her TV. Duchess laughed as she made her way to the bedroom and sat on her bed. Walking in behind her, I closed the door.

"Can we talk now?" I said, slapping my hands together. The look on her face was so nonchalant. She was looking at her phone, completely and utterly ignoring me. "Duchess!"

"What? Now what in the hell do you want, Yaheem?" she said, rolling her eyes. I snatched her phone and stuffed it in my pants pocket.

"You gone hear me out, dammit!" I said raising my voice. She gave me the look of a child and sat there in silence.

"Okay, fine. Talk then."

"Now, I'm tired of playing games with you, you know where I stand, okay? Just because I don't say love, doesn't mean I don't feel that way. It just goes deeper than that. I'm not frontin' right now, for real."

"Okay, how deep then? Let me hear it." I sighed and sat on the floor next to her bed. "The reason why is because, my ex, that bitch was the love of my life. We was fucking with each other heavy for years. I was going to marry that bitch. Have kids with her. Until she cheated and was only using me for my money. I begged and begged for her to stay with me like a simp ass nigga, but she ain't love me, she never did.

"A nigga poured his heart out. Said that love shit to the wrong person and got fucked up over it. I don't know how many times, and she just walked out of my life. Like a blink of an eye, she was gone. And now she hooked on drugs. A fucking crack head. I don't think that will happen with you. I just need time to say those words. I want that shit to make you feel like you on cloud nine, just give me time." She sat there in silence. Until she broke out in laughter.

"Wow. So, you thought that was going to fix this? Such a sad story. You're fucking joking, right?" I looked at her crazy.

"I'm dead serious, why would I lie? About some shit like that? That bitch aborted my baby, conned me to wine and dine her for years, and cheated on me more than once. Niggas supposed to be hard, but that shit broke me," I said, getting upset.

"Cause that shit is so made the fuck up. A guy like you, going through some shit like that? Please. Yaheem, those are player lines and—"

"Shut the fuck up! Duchess, you act all bad and hard and shit, when you just as soft! You cold as fuck, I'm pouring out my heart and you just laugh in my damn face! When you don't get your way, you fucking act like this? All you females is the fucking same. You can keep playing games, fuck this shit, I'm out. Tell that nigga Keon that bullshit ass line and see how he play yo' ass again. Be with that nigga."

"You shut up! And you probably are lying who knows! And at least he loved me, instead of just fucking me! What have you done for me, huh?" I gave her the coldest stare ever.

"What have I done? I did a lot, I saved you! The same nigga that set you up? The same bitch nigga that cheated on you, huh? That nigga better than me? Watch it, don't end up fucked up before you come to reality! Oh, you really think another nigga can cause that pussy to throb the way I do, huh? Every time you see me, you weak at the damn knees, Duchess! Alright then. If he can do you better than me, then shid, you don't need me. All I'm telling you is watch yo' back, because looks can be deceiving. And Keon is full of it. But yo' stubborn ass can't see it. Do me a favor and lose my number," I said as I pointed between us and waved my finger.

"This? Us? It's over, shorty." Before Duchess could say a word back. I walked out of the room and told Trigga to bring his ass. Something vibrated in my pocket, and I remembered I had her phone. I looked at it and froze.

"Aye, baby girl. Just wanted to tell you good night, you mean so much to me. I can't wait for you to give me that call so I can give you what you been missing, and I love you always. I enjoyed the kiss the other night, hope you did too…" My face grew tight with anger.

"What's up, my boy? Why you looking like that?" Trigga questioned. I clutched the phone and busted into her room, throwing the phone against the hardwood floor as it shattered.

"Tell that nigga Keon you love him! Man, I'm through with yo' ass." She came flying out of her room behind me as she gave me a look, screaming.

"What the fuck, my phone!" Duchess yelled. Trigga held her back. Before she could even explain, I held my hand up to stop her.

I chuckled a bit. "And to think I did have a thing for you bad *and* did *love* you! Man, fuck this shit. And *did* being the key word! Bye, I'm out this bitch. Duchess, have a nice fucking life." I walked out, slamming the door. Trigga was right behind me as I made it to the car.

"Come on, nigga!" He was shocked and hopped in the car.

"Man, you really gone break up with her?" he said, using his thumb to point back towards the house.

"She kissed another nigga. I don't know what else happened. I'm done with her with her bullshit." I pulled off as I burnt rubber, turning the corner. Wasted my time for nothing.

Chapter 17

Keon

Getting back to my house, I felt good. The relationship was ruined, and I was in a good place. Everything I did worked, and he was in the streets with hoes around him. I laid down on the soft sofa and closed my eyes. Only to feel a body lay on top of my chest. "What, girl?" I said as I peeped my eyes open.

"If your bitch hit me again. I'ma end her ass. I've been nice for too long and did what you told me. Now get rid of that bitch Duchess." I groaned and fully looked down to get a glimpse of her. She was in nothing but a Calvin Klein thong and cropped tank that exposed her big breasts. "Man, Candice. You don't move unless I say so," I said while slapping her fat ass. Her blue hair was wild and in a messy bun and that eye was still a little black and swollen.

"Nah, I'm sick of that hoe, and if you think about fucking her, I'ma beat yo ass. This my dick," Candice whined. She thought I was hers, but that shit was a lie. Licking my lips, I grabbed her face and kissed her big lips.

"Yo' ass will live. You gotta learn how to bob and weave, girl," I said chuckling. She slapped me on my face and leaned up and kissed me as she squeezed my face. "Man, you gone stop hitting me." I rubbed the back of my cheek, shit stung like a bitch.

"Just get rid of the little bitch already. Now come here. I want to suck this dick," she said as she slid down to my crotch and pulled down my sweatpants.

"Go 'head, then," I said, licking my lips as I bit on my bottom lip. A sensation shot up my body as I felt her warm mouth on my dick. Candice started going crazy with her wet throat as I thought of Duchess. I was going do what the fuck I planned. Candice couldn't rush the plan or tell me what to do, when I was going to get what was rightfully mine...

***

Yaheem

"Where's my money? You've owed me for the past few months now. I'm not the one to be fucked with. You for sure should know that."

"I-I know. But I'm trying to get all your money, Yaheem," she said, looking down. She looked too young to even be on drugs.

"It's Versace to you. Look at you, bruh. Chaz, how many times do I have to tell you to stay off these streets and get some damn help! You're the number one out hea' buying and fucking dudes for your next fix." I looked at my ex with dark eyes.

"I know, Versace, I'm trying! Ever since I got with that guy, it's been downhill from there. I thought it was love but he only turned me out. I'm sorry—"

"Man, I don't even want to hear that bruh, I don't care about none of that shit you spitting. Ain't no going back. You left me for a junkie. Blah, blah, blah... I'ma let your ass slide once again. I want my money! Don't play with me, Chaz. Get my shit! Now get the fuck on." She nodded and I shooed her away. It was sad to see her that way, but these streets are hard. She let a nun' ass nigga turn her out. I shook my thoughts of her away. I needed to get my ass home and off the cold ass streets. I made my last sale and hopped in my car, pulling off.

I ain't turn no music on, I just wanted it silent. For some reason, my brother Voshon popped into my head. I really missed him, that was my only brother and he's gone, because of some sick bastard who shot and hung him on the streets of

NOLA. I'll never forget that day of pure hell. My momma well she slipped into depression and hasn't been right ever since. My pops, he ran off long ago. So ever since my brother got murdered, I been on my own. Making it the best way I could, hitting the block every day, grinding and making my way. Praying along the way. The streets were my only way to survive. It was the only thing I knew in this world.

As my mind wondered about my life. I pulled into my driveway and parked my ride. I got out and made sure it was locked. I turned my hat to the back as I let myself in. When I entered my quiet home, I threw my keys on the counter and went into the living room. I fell back on the couch and turned on my TV. My phone buzzed like five times.

I saw it was an unknown number. licking my lips and hitting the green button as I put the phone to my ear. "What's the word, who this?" I questioned through the phone. "Hello!"

"Please, Yaheem, let's just talk this out. I'm using my old ass iPhone 11 right now and the bitch gone die soon. Let's just talk—" Hanging up the phone soon as I heard her voice, I threw the phone next to me and stared off into space. I ain't want to talk to her. It buzzed again and I groaned. I wasn't even going to look at it, I ain't want to talk whatsoever. I had too much on my mind anyway.

My phone buzzed once more, and it was pissing me off so I looked at it. And I wish I hadn't. "Yaheem, have you seen Duchess' sex tape with Keon?" My eyes stared at that message from another unknown number. She fucked him too? Can't believe she cheated on me when we was "together."

Monet Dragun

Chapter 18

Duchess

It's so boring being here by myself, man. It's been weeks and that busted iPhone 11 was not working for shit. The battery was so fucked. I was glad my new phone had just come in and I called up Yaheem, but he was not trying to hear shit that coming from me once again. Keon keeps calling me and texting me, but I don't wanna deal with him. My phone rang again, and I looked down at it. It was my mom again. but just like I did the last time she called, I started to hang up. But deep inside, I wanted to know what she wanted, so this time I answered.

"Hello?" I said through the phone. It took her a minute before she responded.

"Hello, Duchess. How's life going for you?" she asked.

"Robin, listen, what do you want? I know you don't care about how me or how my life is going, you never did," I said coldly to her.

"Watch who you're talking to, little girl. At the end of the damn day, I'm still your fucking mother. You think you're grown cause you strip? You're a slut! That's why I kicked you out. You think you're the shit now cause you moved into that luxury apartment?" Robin said. My mother was a twisted bitch, I didn't understand why she was like this, and I didn't care to know now.

"Lady, why are you calling me? You didn't care about me. You didn't care when I was under your roof! Bitch, you looked over them kids before me, you didn't give a shit about me ever since my daddy got killed! You let your blood get beat on and raped by a nigga you call your husband. You ain't no mama, we were just checks to you. The fuck, Robin! You ain't no mama and you never gave a fuck about me! Don't call my phone no more, fuck you!" I hung up the phone and threw it on the couch in my room. This was too much, who did she think she was? A mom? She was never a mom to me, ever.

"This shit is too much," I said to myself. I just decided to watch one of my favorite movies, *Set It Off.* It would help me get back into my happy place. One of my favorite all-time movies, that and *Poetic Justice.* The 90s movies were a thing to bring back some goof memories, and that was what I needed right now. As I got comfortable, my phone rang as it blasted "Bloodstain" by SZA. Taking me away from my movie which had just started, I picked it up and it was Yaheem, my heart thumped as I quickly answered.

"H-Hi—" I couldn't finish before he cut me off.

"Please, don't tell me you made a damn sex tape with Keon! Some nigga or bitch is texting my phone with this bull-shit. All I seen was ass shaking on dick, and believe me, I know that ass. And pictures of you when you was at the club, but nothing with him. But the video, yeah. This nigga is trying to ruin your life, can't you see that shit?" I looked at the phone in shock.

"So, he is trying to ruin my fucking life. That was when we were dating, and I didn't know he had that. I deleted it from his phone, that shit was private. No one can even tell it's me. There's no face and you can only hear him! Now, I'm sorry for what I did and everything. I have issues and taking it out on you ain't right."

"Yeah man, this shit is a lot, it's whatever though." I rolled my eyes. And ignored his comment. I was about to say something to him, when there was a loud knock at my front door.

"Uh, hold on. Someone is knocking on my door. I wasn't expecting anyone. Maybe it the pizza I ordered."

"Ight. I'll wait." I nodded as if he could see me and laid my phone down on the bed, while it was still on the charger. I threw on my big t-shirt and went downstairs to the door. I skipped down the steps. The person kept banging on my door like the damn police.

"Ugh! Hol' up!" I unlocked the door and opened it without even thinking. I was met with my number-one enemy. "What the fuck are you doing here, and how did you find out where I the fuck I live?" I questioned when I saw the person before me. My blood curdled and my mind spun. And it flashed back to the time when this exact same person tried to hurt me.

"Bitch, just shut up!" the dirty rough voice shouted in my face as they kept the gun in place. And proceeded to try and strip my clothes from me. As he kept this up, I squirmed and disobeyed. This was not about to happen again. No, no, no!

"I'm going to tell my mommy! You don't know who y'all actually fucking with!" I yelled at the old man, but he punched me in the stomach. Sending me in a world of pain. Knocking the window out of my system. Causing me to curl up in pain. But I brought everything up in me to knee him in his junk.

"You stupid bitch!" The man backhanded me, but I was not about to go out like a scared puppy. I head butted him and kicked him in the stomach. Someone grabbed ahold of my neck, and I was sent into a tiff of struggles.

"Lemme go! Lemme g-go!" I screamed, my vision became blurry, and I tried not to black out. It was not my damn time to go. I mustered every ounce of energy in me and screamed. "Mommy, help me please! Let me go, you're my o-own blood!" I screeched.

"We ain't fucking blood, hoe!" He squeezed harder and bent down towards me, his nasty tongue licking across my face.

"You're sick, Charles! Get away from me!"

"Hello?" He said as he snapped in my face.

"The fuck are you doing here, leave!" He coughed and fixed his jacket.

"I just needed t-to tell you something." I looked at him with disgust.

"Nigga, I have a Glock, don't make me use it! Choose your words wisely." He sighed.

"I know what—"

"Shut the hell up and tell me what the fuck you gotta say." He coughed again, harder this time. Holding his chest in the process. "I'm dying and I just want to apologize for the shit I did to you. And I just want to let you know that everything I've done was due to your mom. She told me to do whatever..." he broke off into a fit of coughs and wheezing. "Whatever the fuck I wanted for her money, you were the sugar to her fix."

"You're lying, how did you even find my out where I lived? Get away from here before I call the damn police! Now!"

"I'm telling you the truth. It's some shit that ain't going right with her anymore. Someone came talking to her about your dad and his death. She said you were the one that killed him. Put the gun in your hand and made you fire it like a toy." I slammed the door in his face and ran upstairs with tears in my eyes. This can't be true, it can't be. I saw Yaheem was still on the phone. I picked it up and debated if I should hang up or talk to him.

"H-hello," I croaked.

"Uh, what's wrong? It took you forever, you good?" His voice sent me into a spiral. I was crying uncontrollably.

"Yaheem, all these years I thought my life was just pointless because of my mother, when it was just me. I could have did so much in my fucking life. I'm so sick, she did this shit to me. I could have been the one who killed my dad, due to my mom. All the lies she put in my head about how he died in the streets because of someone who set him up. When it was me, and she put the gun in my hand to do it… I can't take this, it's always something! First my daddy gets taken from me, then I was raped, my life is just a wreck! I shouldn't even be here, all those times I tried to kill myself and it didn't work, maybe this time it will."

"Wait! Stop all that crazy talk—"

"No! I wanted to fix us, but I can't even fix my damn self! I can't do this shit anymore, goodbye, Yaheem." I hung up the phone when he was in mid-sentence. This shit was sickening, my life was hell, I fucked up my relationship. What else can go wrong, what else!

I went into my bathroom and pulled the pills out of my cabinet. I looked at them as tears streamed down my face. I thought what my life would've been like if my dad was still alive, I would not be in this situation I am today. "What are you thinking, Duchess..." I opened one bottle and looked at the red pills. Maybe this will solve everything. I rolled my head back as the pills entered my mouth one by one.

Monet Dragun

Chapter 19

Yaheem

Saving a soul, that can't be saved. I was in full panic. I pulled on my jogging pants, halfway falling down, trying to get one leg in at a time. I didn't care if I didn't have any boxers on. *I had to see about Duchess.* She was talkin' reckless, and I wasn't feeling that shit. I ran out of my house slamming the door hard. So hard I might've broken something. I dashed across the grass and put my key into the lock, frantically trying to get it open. My nerves were so frazzled.

I finally got it unlocked and put my key into the ignition. The car kept dying on me. "C'mon baby, not now, please start up!" In frustration, I slammed on the steering wheel repeatedly. "C'mon, c'mon!" With all my praying and pleading, the car started up. I put the car in reverse and put the pedal to the metal and backed out, creating black tire marks on my pavement.

I swirled out of the driveway and sped down the street, swerving and blowing my horn like a mad man. Trying to get anything and everyone out of my way. *Duchess needs me.*

"Watch where you're going, asshole!" some old hag yelled out of her window.

"Shut cho' ass up, looking like a goon!" I was heading down the interstate now.

"Why the hell do she have to live so far!" I yelled to myself. Sweat was pouring down the side of my "self-made" tattoos. My breathing was heavy, and my heart was damn near about to burst out of my chest at any moment.

In a panic, I picked up my phone and scrolled through my contacts, trying to find her number. I found her contact while trying to keep my eyes on the road. I hit the call button and pressed the phone against my ear. "C'mon girl, answer the damn phone!" I screamed.

The phone rang and rang. I couldn't lose her this way. She deserved to be in this world. Her life and heart was so damaged. She needed to be healed. And this wasn't the way. My nerves calmed as I heard her sweet voice. But my heart broke a string as her voice was so dry and lifeless.

"I'm s-so, sorry, Y-Yaheem. I-I never meant to..." The line went dead, and my heart nearly fell out of my chest.

"Duchess! Duchess! Stay on this phone, you're not leaving me!" I could hear ha' gasping for air and wheezing. "Duchess! Baby, I love you without a doubt, stay with me!"

Yaheem, you won't regret those three words. She needs you.

"Y-Yaheem!" her dying voice screeched into the phone. Something wasn't right, God something else is happening over there. Then out of nowhere I heard Duchess screaming, then the sounds of glass breaking, and the sounds of a fight. A male was yelling, and I couldn't tell who it was. Duchess was screaming and gasping, and the fighting grew more frantic.

The male's muffled voice came through the phone, "You dumb bitch!" But I couldn't tell who it was.

"Baby! Talk to me, who's there!" I screamed, slamming my hand on my steering wheel. I slammed onto my brakes when some idiot pulled in front of me. A lot of ruffling was covering what was going on making my heart pound even harder.

"Duch—" the phone went completely dead, and I lost it. Tears streamed down my eyes, and I pulled around the person as they skirted off. I looked in their car as we passed and it was that bitch Blu. Fuck was she doing all the way over here?

That was something I'd figure that out later...

I ran every damn red light, not giving a damn about any-one, but *Duchess*. "I'm coming, Duchess! I'm almost there!" I screamed to myself. I dialed her number again and it went straight to voicemail. I made a major turn onto her street, with my car pushing ninety miles per hour. When I saw her house, I hit the brakes hard, making my car jump forward. I snatched the seat belt off and ran up the path to her door.

I kicked that door down and ran up down the hall to her bedroom. I busted into her room, only for her not to be there. I looked around as sweat drenched my shirt. "Duchess! Duch-ess!" I yelled, trying to get her to respond to me. I ran my hands through my hair, almost pulling it out. I cursed myself out for not getting here faster, to stop her from harming herself and catching whoever was in this house. Who had attacked her?

A breeze rushed by me, and I knew that feeling all too well. Something told me to look out of her porch window. I dipped around her bed and pulled her curtains, making me al-most break down. Duchess was lying face down in the pool. "Oh my God!" I slammed the glass door to the left, hearing it shatter completely as I ran outside. I tossed my hat and phone onto the grass and dived into the pool, swimming towards her lifeless body. I grabbed her and pulled her to the edge. "Wake up! Baby, I love you, wake up! Wake up, please!" I tapped her face she was so cold. C'mon, Yaheem, where is your damn mind!

I put my index and thumb on her nose, pinching it shut, I tilted her head back and opened her mouth, putting my lips against hers, blowing air into her body three times. I looked at her icy blue lips and put both of my hands on her chest pushing down four times. "One... two... three... four, breathe, baby! Please!" I did this horrifying act six times in a row, but she wasn't responding.

"C'mon, Duchess, gahdammit! I ain't losing you! I'm not!" I pulled her close to me and rocked back and forth, shaking her. Hoping she'd wake up. "Don't leave me like my brother left me! Please, j-just wake up... I-I love you." Hot tears rolled down my face as I looked down at her cold, wet lifeless body. I picked her up, like a groom carrying a bride, and took her to where my phone was, dialing 9-1-1. I can't lose her. God knows I can't...

Chapter 20

Duchess

I could hear Yaheem's footsteps running towards me. The water continued to fill my lungs as everything around me was muffled. *"Oh, damn! What the fuck! Baby, what happened? Oh fuck, fuck, there's so much blood in the pool!"* Yaheem *said, before he dived into the pool, grabbing my limp body and dragging me from the water. "C'mon, Duchess, gahdammit! What they do to you? I ain't losing you! I'm not!"* Yaheem *shouted as he laid me flat on the grass. He began to perform CPR as he pressed his strong hands against my chest. "One, two, three, c'mon!"*
Yaheem kept doing the action nonstop, not giving up on me. "Fuck, please c'mon! Wake up, cough the water up, baby please! Just come back to me, you're bleeding everywhere!" He didn't stop till finally, I violently coughed up some of the water. Yaheem pulled me close to him and rocked back and forth shaking me. "Don't leave me like my brother left me! Please, j-just wake up... I-I love you..." My eyes opened and I lifted up, looking dead at him.
"Yaheem, I love you too, baby. I'm... wait, what?" He was still crying and shaking me. "Yaheem, I'm awake!" I yelled at him. Trying to touch his face, my hand went right through him.
"No, I can't be!" I looked down at myself and I was still laying there. Not responding to anything he was saying. He was now on the phone, yelling at the paramedics to get here. He tried CPR once again, but I wasn't moving. I can't be dead! I just can't be. I looked as he got even worse, breaking down at the seams. I looked into the house, something just told me to go into that house.

I looked back at myself and Yaheem, what we could've been. The love we could've had, the life we could've lived, the power couple we could've been. He really didn't want to lose me. I stepped over all the glass and looked at the scene. The pill bottle, the broken items on my dresser, the shattered mirror, bloody handprints, and blood smeared everywhere. Everything that happened before I ended up in that pool. But one thing was missing... The person who did this to me.

I blinked and I saw another version of myself, fending for my life. His hands wrapped around my neck. Strangling the life out of me and slinging my body around like a doll. I was already incoherent from the some of the pills that slipped down my throat.

I was too scared to take them all, too scared to off myself because I knew I had a life to live. I couldn't take my own life. I just couldn't do it. It's so many people who love me and care for my well-being I just couldn't be selfish. But this man who had so much hate because I didn't want him, wanted me dead. It wasn't Blu. It wasn't Shanice, my ex-best friend.

It was the man I had rejected over and over, Keon, the man who swore he loved me so much. He ripped off his black ski mask, revealing himself to me.

"Keon! G-get off of me!" I screamed weakly. He threw me into my dresser and mirror as glass flew everywhere. I screamed in pain as the glass sliced through my skin. He had the darkest look in his eyes as he stomped over to me and picked me up as I screamed. He tossed me on the bed as I whimpered.

"Bitch, now it's your time to die!" His grip around my neck got tighter and tighter. As I watched what happened to me, I could faintly hear the ambulance coming towards my apartment. Tears filled my shadowy eyes as I watched me struggle for dear life once again.

I looked behind me and Yaheem was still holding me as the paramedics came into my backyard. I looked back into my out-of-body experience. Keon was still on top of me, but I was fighting back with the ounce of strength I had left. My phone started to ring, and I desperately struggled to get it. Pressed the answer button. Thank God! It was Yaheem...
"Yaheem, you gotta help me! They tryna kill me, he in the house! Stop, get away from me! I never meant for this to happen, no!"
"Duchess! Duchess!" *Keon snatched the phone away.*
"He ain't gone help you this time... I would've gave you the fucking world!"
"Duchess, who's there with you?" *Yaheem screamed through the phone. Keon laughed as my breathing became less and less.*
"K—" *he threw my phone against the wall, shattering it. He pressed his hands around my neck. Plunging my neck and head, deeper and deeper into the bed, making me see stars. I nearly blacked out. But he wasn't done. He made sure I was still coming too. I watched as this sick bastard groped my body and picked me up, taking my now limp body outside. He threw me into the pool. I put my hand up to my mouth as I cried out. No one could hear me. I was only in spirit.*
"No one will save you, bitch! Not even Yaheem..." *My body rose to the surface as I laid face down in the pool. I screamed out, why was this happening to me? Something always happens to me. Keon turned around with a grim look on his face and walked back towards the house. Walking straight through my body. He picked up my phone and chucked it into the pool with me. No evidence if it was destroyed. I had to live, I needed to survive. Things just couldn't end this way, I just can't go out like this. The need to get back to Yaheem was my*

fuel to live, I had something to live on this earth for, and it was love.

***

Yaheem

"What do you mean, she's brain dead! Go in there and save her! I'm not pulling no damn plug, I'm not killin' her, I love her!" The doctor looked at me with sadness.

"We're doing everything possible..." A cold grave wind flew past me, and I looked around. I looked in the hospital room window and she was still laying there... *Lifeless... Come on, baby, you can make it!* I thought.

"Yaheem! Yaheem!" I heard someone yell. I turned around to be met with a fist to my face. Trigga tried to pull him off of me. But I was mad, and he was too.

"You caused this shit! Now my damn sister laying in that bed half-dead!" he yelled, punching me in the stomach. I winced in pain and threw my arm back, putting all my might into the punch to his jaw. He went flying to the ground and I hemmed his ass up.

"I ain't cause this! I was trying to save her, I love her. I love that girl, fuck! You need to worry about her, instead of trying to fight me, the wrong person!" He bit his tongue and didn't say a word back. I stood up and fixed myself. Trigga tried to say something to me, but I was tuning everyone out. Tears poured out of my eyes when I saw that damn flat red line. I smacked my palm on the window, screaming her name.

"Duchess, nah, you can't go! Don't leave me! You was the love I needed, I thought I was the man you could trust!" Something white stood over her and looked at me dead in my face. A smile appeared on her face, and I was stunned. The figure got into bed and laid on top of her body, disappearing. Another figure appeared in the room and waved at me.

It was Voshon... I couldn't believe what I was seeing. I almost passed out from the sight. God was watching us... Before I could muster the words, "I miss you," he disappeared. A beeping noise pulled me out of my sorrows, it was her monitor. She wasn't moving yet. But that green line went up and down. That was good enough for me.

She wasn't leaving me not yet... not ever.

Monet Dragun

Chapter 21

Yaheem

Sitting in the seat next to her bed, I stared at her lovely frame. I had my head rest on bout of my fist. Her chest heaved up and down, as she inhaled and exhaled. The heart monitor went up and down. The regulator went up and down, the sounds of the hospital were getting to me. Her brother was in here earlier, he was so mad he wasn't here to protect her.

I was mad at myself that I didn't. My thoughts were broken when the door softly opened. "Yes?" I said as I looked at her doctor.

"Um, sir, can I talk to you privately? It's urgent." I nodded and got up, but before I left out of the room, I kissed her forehead softly. "Love you." I stuffed my hand in my pockets and walked out the door with the doctor. He got straight to the information.

"Um, is her last name spelled Harold? Or Hollon?" he questioned as he looked at her chart.

"What! Her last name is neither of those. Her last name is Lewis, Doctor Harris," I said, rubbing my forehead. I can't believe these people got her shit mixed up.

He sighed deeply and slammed the papers down on the counter. "I can't believe they did this! The nurse that filed this is going to get fired. I'm so sorry for this improper mix up, I really am. She *is* not brain dead, but there is something you need to know. Unfortunately, though… she is pregnant, and this could be life threatening to the baby. But we are doing everything we can do. Did you know she was pregnant?" My eyes widened and I almost lost my balance.

"Sir, Mr. Carter, are you alright?" he asked.

"Y-yeah? Is the baby o-okay?" He nodded.

"The baby is fine, but Duchess is still fighting for her life. We're keeping her on life support as long as we can. We're hoping she doesn't slip into a coma while she is pregnant. That won't be good because she is only six weeks pregnant. Too early in her pregnancy. Mr. Carter, we are doing the best we can.

"And I know taking her off of life support is not in the equation. So, here we are doing everything we can for them, we will put Duchess in a medically induced coma. This will not affect the baby. But we are monitoring her for the baby's sake. At this point it's all up to Duchess. But we can't guarantee anything. I'm sorry..." It felt like my heart had been ripped out of my chest and stepped on several times. I couldn't say anything, I couldn't gather the words.

"Mr. Carter?" he questioned, as he put his hand on my shoulder.

"Y-yeah?" I said, holding back tears.

"She is going to be fine. We're going to do everything possible. Just listen, Mr. Carter, this is going to be hard for her. She had a lot of trauma, whoever did this made sure she'd end up here. I've seen a lot of cases like this, this beautiful woman was put through a lot. And from what we can tell as of right now, it's all on her now. That's all I can give you, sir. Please pray for her, it's in God's hands now." I nodded and just looked at Duchess through the glass window. I wanted her to just wake up and hug and kiss me. I wanted to hold her and tell her much I needed her. "Baby, just come back to me please..."

***

Duchess

162

I'm going to be a mommy! And I'm laying in this bed half fucking dead. I can't believe this happened to me. I'm going to wake up from this a new woman! I'm going to take my life back, I'm going to live, I'm going to live, I'm going to live!

A bright light came down from the heavens and a man walked through the light. I didn't know who this man was. "Um, who are you?" *I questioned.*

"I'm Voshon, Yaheem's brother. And this is—" *he picked up a beautiful baby girl and cradled her in her arms.* "And this is your baby girl..." *Tears ran down my face and I held my hand against my mouth.*

"This is your baby girl..." *he said straightforward. I couldn't stop crying, I just couldn't.*

"How? Wait—"

"Just shh, you have a choice. Either you cross the threshold and go to judgement with God. Or you go back and be in a coma for a few weeks, and fight for your baby and Yaheem," *he said to me as he passed me the beautiful baby girl who was sucking her thumb.*

"I can't leave him or this baby! Voshon, help me. I'm dying, how am I supposed to hold on?" *He pointed to me, and Yaheem was holding my hand, praying and kissing me. He was putting my hand on my stomach, rubbing it. Tears were running down his cheeks and I wanted to hold him, touch him, kiss him.*

"Baby, please... Come back to me, I need you. Don't leave like she did. I do love you..." *I looked down at the baby, her big brown eyes were staring up at me.*

"So, do you want to go through those gates or stay?" *I looked from Voshon to the baby.*

"I want to go back! Please, I need to!" *The baby disappeared out of my hands and so did Voshon. I was by myself.*

"Voshon, Voshon!" I dropped to my knees and cried. Someone touched my shoulder and I looked up to see a grown, older man. "Dad?" I said with tears in my eyes

"Baby girl, you can't stay, go back. I know you needed me for all those years. But trust me, I was always there in your heart. None of this was your fault, you didn't kill me...greed is what killed me. Robin will get the karma that's come for her. I love you... And I miss you. I never meant to leave you... You'll find out the truth. Bye, Duchess, my love. I'll see you soon but not now." He disappeared too and I was left with myself and Yaheem. I touched her face and kissed his lips. "I want to go back... God, I need this."

Everything that was white, pure, and beautiful vanished. It was just Yaheem beside me, and he squeezed my hand. It was warm, his touch was radiating through me, but I couldn't move. I just wanted to move and hold him. Yaheem stared down at me, then he leaned in closer as he kissed my cheek repeatedly. Out of nowhere, I was starting to feel something, his love was saving me, that's what I thought. My hand started to twitch at the sensation. But that was it, nothing else. I still couldn't talk, move, or open my eyes, but I could feel Yaheem beside me.

"Duchess, I knew you wasn't going to leave me. I can just feel it. I promise, the nigga who did this is going to get his..."

"I know..." I said in my head.

"Sir, visiting hours are over. Sorry, but you'll need to leave in a few," a soft voice hummed. Yaheem looked around to the short, stacked nurse.

"Nah, I'm not leaving her side. So just get me a blanket, Nurse." The nurse didn't say a word, she just nodded and walked out as she closed the door. "I'm not leaving your side ever again. I promise you that. It's gone be us against the world, like I said from the jump, baby. You can trust me. Duchess, just come back and I promise, a nigga got you," Ya-heem said with a sniffle as he rubbed my belly. "You all I got..."

"Lord, please bring me back to him, please. I believe in your will and power, Father God. Just give me one more chance to make us right again. In a hustler I trust... amen."

To Be Continued...
In a Hustler I Trust 2
Coming Soon

Lock Down Publications and Ca$h Presents assisted publishing packages.

BASIC PACKAGE $499
Editing
Cover Design
Formatting

UPGRADED PACKAGE $800
Typing
Editing
Cover Design
Formatting

ADVANCE PACKAGE $1,200
Typing
Editing
Cover Design
Formatting
Copyright registration
Proofreading
Upload book to Amazon

LDP SUPREME PACKAGE $1,500
Typing
Editing
Cover Design
Formatting
Copyright registration
Proofreading

Set up Amazon account
Upload book to Amazon
Advertise on LDP Amazon and Facebook page

***Other services available upon request. Additional charges may apply
Lock Down Publications
P.O. Box 944
Stockbridge, GA 30281-9998
Phone # 470 303-9761

Submission Guideline

Submit the first three chapters of your completed manuscript to ldpsubmissions@gmail.com, subject line: Your book's title. The manuscript must be in a .doc file and sent as an attachment. Document should be in Times New Roman, double spaced and in size 12 font. Also, provide your synopsis and full contact information. If sending multiple submissions, they must each be in a separate email.

Have a story but no way to send it electronically? You can still submit to LDP/Ca$h Presents. Send in the first three chapters, written or typed, of your completed manuscript to:

LDP: Submissions Dept
Po Box 944
Stockbridge, Ga 30281

DO NOT send original manuscript. Must be a duplicate.

Provide your synopsis and a cover letter containing your full contact information.

Thanks for considering LDP and Ca$h Presents.

<u>NEW RELEASES</u>

KING OF THE TRENCHES 2 by GHOST & TRANAY
ADAMS
MOB TIES 5 by SAYNOMORE
KING KILLA by VINCENT "VITTO" HOLLOWAY
JACK BOYS VS DOPE BOYS by ROMELL TUKES
KILLA KOUNTY 2 by KHUFU
IN A HUSTLER I TRUST by MONET DRAGUN

BLOOD OF A BOSS **VI**

SHADOWS OF THE GAME II

TRAP BASTARD II

By **Askari**

LOYAL TO THE GAME **IV**

By **T.J. & Jelissa**

IF TRUE SAVAGE **VIII**

MIDNIGHT CARTEL IV

DOPE BOY MAGIC IV

CITY OF KINGZ III

NIGHTMARE ON SILENT AVE II

THE PLUG OF LIL MEXICO II

By **Chris Green**

BLAST FOR ME **III**

A SAVAGE DOPEBOY III

CUTTHROAT MAFIA III

DUFFLE BAG CARTEL VII

HEARTLESS GOON VI

By **Ghost**

A HUSTLER'S DECEIT III

KILL ZONE II

BAE BELONGS TO ME III

By **Aryanna**

KING OF THE TRAP III

By **T.J. Edwards**

GORILLAZ IN THE BAY V

3X KRAZY III

STRAIGHT BEAST MODE II

De'Kari

KINGPIN KILLAZ IV

STREET KINGS III

PAID IN BLOOD III

CARTEL KILLAZ IV

DOPE GODS III

Hood Rich

SINS OF A HUSTLA II

ASAD

RICH $AVAGE II

MONEY IN THE GRAVE II

By Martell Troublesome Bolden

YAYO V

Bred In The Game 2

S. Allen

CREAM III

By Yolanda Moore

SON OF A DOPE FIEND III

HEAVEN GOT A GHETTO II

By Renta

LOYALTY AIN'T PROMISED III

By Keith Williams

I'M NOTHING WITHOUT HIS LOVE II

SINS OF A THUG II

TO THE THUG I LOVED BEFORE II

IN A HUSTLER I TRUST II

By Monet Dragun

QUIET MONEY IV

EXTENDED CLIP III

THUG LIFE IV

By **Trai'Quan**

THE STREETS MADE ME IV

By **Larry D. Wright**

IF YOU CROSS ME ONCE II

By **Anthony Fields**

THE STREETS WILL NEVER CLOSE II

By K'ajji

HARD AND RUTHLESS III

THE BILLIONAIRE BENTLEYS II

Von Diesel

KILLA KOUNTY III

By Khufu

MONEY GAME III

By Smoove Dolla

JACK BOYS VS DOPE BOYS II

By Romell Tukes

MURDA WAS THE CASE II

Elijah R. Freeman

THE STREETS NEVER LET GO II

By Robert Baptiste

AN UNFORESEEN LOVE III

By **Meesha**

KING OF THE TRENCHES III
by **GHOST & TRANAY ADAMS**

MONEY MAFIA II
LOYAL TO THE SOIL II
By **Jibril Williams**
QUEEN OF THE ZOO II
By **Black Migo**
THE BRICK MAN IV
By King Rio
VICIOUS LOYALTY II
By Kingpen
A GANGSTA'S PAIN II
By J-Blunt
CONFESSIONS OF A JACKBOY III
By Nicholas Lock
GRIMEY WAYS II
By Ray Vinci
KING KILLA II
By Vincent "Vitto" Holloway

Available Now

RESTRAINING ORDER **I & II**
By **CA$H & Coffee**
LOVE KNOWS NO BOUNDARIES **I II & III**

By **Coffee**
RAISED AS A GOON I, II, III & IV
BRED BY THE SLUMS I, II, III
BLAST FOR ME I & II
ROTTEN TO THE CORE I II III
A BRONX TALE I, II, III
DUFFLE BAG CARTEL I II III IV V VI
HEARTLESS GOON I II III IV V
A SAVAGE DOPEBOY I II
DRUG LORDS I II III
CUTTHROAT MAFIA I II
KING OF THE TRENCHES
By **Ghost**
LAY IT DOWN **I & II**
LAST OF A DYING BREED I II
BLOOD STAINS OF A SHOTTA I & II III
By **Jamaica**
LOYAL TO THE GAME I II III
LIFE OF SIN I, II III
By **TJ & Jelissa**
BLOODY COMMAS I & II
SKI MASK CARTEL I II & III
KING OF NEW YORK I II,III IV V
RISE TO POWER I II III
COKE KINGS I II III IV V
BORN HEARTLESS I II III IV
KING OF THE TRAP I II

By **T.J. Edwards**

IF LOVING HIM IS WRONG...I & II

LOVE ME EVEN WHEN IT HURTS I II III

By **Jelissa**

WHEN THE STREETS CLAP BACK I & II III

THE HEART OF A SAVAGE I II III

MONEY MAFIA

LOYAL TO THE SOIL

By **Jibril Williams**

A DISTINGUISHED THUG STOLE MY HEART I II & III

LOVE SHOULDN'T HURT I II III IV

RENEGADE BOYS I II III IV

PAID IN KARMA I II III

SAVAGE STORMS I II

AN UNFORESEEN LOVE I II

By **Meesha**

A GANGSTER'S CODE I &, II III

A GANGSTER'S SYN I II III

THE SAVAGE LIFE I II III

CHAINED TO THE STREETS I II III

BLOOD ON THE MONEY I II III

A GANGSTA'S PAIN

By **J-Blunt**

PUSH IT TO THE LIMIT

By **Bre' Hayes**

BLOOD OF A BOSS **I, II, III, IV, V**

SHADOWS OF THE GAME

175

TRAP BASTARD

By **Askari**

THE STREETS BLEED MURDER **I, II & III**

THE HEART OF A GANGSTA I II& III

By **Jerry Jackson**

CUM FOR ME I II III IV V VI VII VIII

An **LDP Erotica Collaboration**

BRIDE OF A HUSTLA **I II & II**

THE FETTI GIRLS **I, II& III**

CORRUPTED BY A GANGSTA I, II III, IV

BLINDED BY HIS LOVE

THE PRICE YOU PAY FOR LOVE I, II ,III

DOPE GIRL MAGIC I II III

By **Destiny Skai**

WHEN A GOOD GIRL GOES BAD

By **Adrienne**

THE COST OF LOYALTY I II III

By Kweli

A GANGSTER'S REVENGE **I II III & IV**

THE BOSS MAN'S DAUGHTERS I II III IV V

A SAVAGE LOVE **I & II**

BAE BELONGS TO ME I II

A HUSTLER'S DECEIT I, II, III

WHAT BAD BITCHES DO I, II, III

SOUL OF A MONSTER I II III

KILL ZONE

A DOPE BOY'S QUEEN I II III

By **Aryanna**

A KINGPIN'S AMBITON

A KINGPIN'S AMBITION **II**

I MURDER FOR THE DOUGH

By **Ambitious**

TRUE SAVAGE I II III IV V VI VII

DOPE BOY MAGIC I, II, III

MIDNIGHT CARTEL I II III

CITY OF KINGZ I II

NIGHTMARE ON SILENT AVE

THE PLUG OF LIL MEXICO II

By **Chris Green**

A DOPEBOY'S PRAYER

By **Eddie "Wolf" Lee**

THE KING CARTEL **I, II & III**

By **Frank Gresham**

THESE NIGGAS AIN'T LOYAL **I, II & III**

By **Nikki Tee**

GANGSTA SHYT **I II &III**

By **CATO**

THE ULTIMATE BETRAYAL

By **Phoenix**

BOSS'N UP **I , II & III**

By **Royal Nicole**

I LOVE YOU TO DEATH

By **Destiny J**

I RIDE FOR MY HITTA
I STILL RIDE FOR MY HITTA
By **Misty Holt**
LOVE & CHASIN' PAPER
By **Qay Crockett**
TO DIE IN VAIN
SINS OF A HUSTLA
By **ASAD**
BROOKLYN HUSTLAZ
By **Boogsy Morina**
BROOKLYN ON LOCK I & II
By **Sonovia**
GANGSTA CITY
By **Teddy Duke**
A DRUG KING AND HIS DIAMOND I & II III
A DOPEMAN'S RICHES
HER MAN, MINE'S TOO I, II
CASH MONEY HO'S
THE WIFEY I USED TO BE I II
By Nicole Goosby
TRAPHOUSE KING **I II & III**
KINGPIN KILLAZ I II III
STREET KINGS I II
PAID IN BLOOD **I II**
CARTEL KILLAZ I II III
DOPE GODS I II
By **Hood Rich**

LIPSTICK KILLAH **I, II, III**

CRIME OF PASSION I II & III

FRIEND OR FOE I II III

By **Mimi**

STEADY MOBBN' **I, II, III**

THE STREETS STAINED MY SOUL I II III

By **Marcellus Allen**

WHO SHOT YA **I, II, III**

SON OF A DOPE FIEND I II

HEAVEN GOT A GHETTO

Renta

GORILLAZ IN THE BAY **I II III IV**

TEARS OF A GANGSTA I II

3X KRAZY I II

STRAIGHT BEAST MODE

DE'KARI

TRIGGADALE I II III

MURDAROBER WAS THE CASE

Elijah R. Freeman

GOD BLESS THE TRAPPERS I, II, III

THESE SCANDALOUS STREETS I, II, III

FEAR MY GANGSTA I, II, III IV, V

THESE STREETS DON'T LOVE NOBODY I, II

BURY ME A G I, II, III, IV, V

A GANGSTA'S EMPIRE I, II, III, IV

THE DOPEMAN'S BODYGAURD I II

THE REALEST KILLAZ I II III

THE LAST OF THE OGS I II III
Tranay Adams
THE STREETS ARE CALLING
Duquie Wilson
MARRIED TO A BOSS I II III
By Destiny Skai & Chris Green
KINGZ OF THE GAME I II III IV V VI
Playa Ray
SLAUGHTER GANG I II III
RUTHLESS HEART I II III
By Willie Slaughter
FUK SHYT
By Blakk Diamond
DON'T F#CK WITH MY HEART I II
By Linnea
ADDICTED TO THE DRAMA I II III
IN THE ARM OF HIS BOSS II
By Jamila
YAYO I II III IV
A SHOOTER'S AMBITION I II
BRED IN THE GAME
By S. Allen
TRAP GOD I II III
RICH $AVAGE
MONEY IN THE GRAVE I II
By Martell Troublesome Bolden
FOREVER GANGSTA

GLOCKS ON SATIN SHEETS I II
By Adrian Dulan
TOE TAGZ I II III
LEVELS TO THIS SHYT I II
By Ah'Million
KINGPIN DREAMS I II III
By Paper Boi Rari
CONFESSIONS OF A GANGSTA I II III IV
CONFESSIONS OF A JACKBOY I II
By Nicholas Lock
I'M NOTHING WITHOUT HIS LOVE
SINS OF A THUG
TO THE THUG I LOVED BEFORE
A GANGSTA SAVED XMAS
IN A HUSTLER I TRUST
By Monet Dragun
CAUGHT UP IN THE LIFE I II III
THE STREETS NEVER LET GO
By Robert Baptiste
NEW TO THE GAME I II III
MONEY, MURDER & MEMORIES I II III
By **Malik D. Rice**
LIFE OF A SAVAGE I II III
A GANGSTA'S QUR'AN I II III
MURDA SEASON I II III
GANGLAND CARTEL I II III
CHI'RAQ GANGSTAS I II III

KILLERS ON ELM STREET I II III

JACK BOYZ N DA BRONX I II III

A DOPEBOY'S DREAM I II III

JACK BOYS VS DOPE BOYS

By **Romell Tukes**

LOYALTY AIN'T PROMISED I II

By Keith Williams

QUIET MONEY I II III

THUG LIFE I II III

EXTENDED CLIP I II

By **Trai'Quan**

THE STREETS MADE ME I II III

By **Larry D. Wright**

THE ULTIMATE SACRIFICE I, II, III, IV, V, VI

KHADIFI

IF YOU CROSS ME ONCE

ANGEL I II

IN THE BLINK OF AN EYE

By **Anthony Fields**

THE LIFE OF A HOOD STAR

By Ca$h & Rashia Wilson

THE STREETS WILL NEVER CLOSE

By K'ajji

CREAM I II

By Yolanda Moore

NIGHTMARES OF A HUSTLA I II III

By King Dream

CONCRETE KILLA I II

VICIOUS LOYALTY

By Kingpen

HARD AND RUTHLESS I II

MOB TOWN 251

THE BILLIONAIRE BENTLEYS

By Von Diesel

GHOST MOB

Stilloan Robinson

MOB TIES I II III IV V

By SayNoMore

BODYMORE MURDERLAND I II III

By Delmont Player

FOR THE LOVE OF A BOSS

By C. D. Blue

MOBBED UP I II III IV

THE BRICK MAN I II III

By King Rio

KILLA KOUNTY I II

By Khufu

MONEY GAME I II

By Smoove Dolla

A GANGSTA'S KARMA I II

By FLAME

KING OF THE TRENCHES I II

by **GHOST & TRANAY ADAMS**

QUEEN OF THE ZOO

By **Black Migo**

GRIMEY WAYS

By Ray Vinci

XMAS WITH AN ATL SHOOTER

By Ca$h & Destiny Skai

KING KILLA

By Vincent "Vitto" Holloway

<u>BOOKS BY LDP'S CEO, CA$H</u>

TRUST IN NO MAN

TRUST IN NO MAN 2

TRUST IN NO MAN 3

BONDED BY BLOOD

SHORTY GOT A THUG

THUGS CRY

THUGS CRY 2

THUGS CRY 3

TRUST NO BITCH

TRUST NO BITCH 2

TRUST NO BITCH 3

TIL MY CASKET DROPS

RESTRAINING ORDER

RESTRAINING ORDER 2

IN LOVE WITH A CONVICT

LIFE OF A HOOD STAR

XMAS WITH AN ATL SHOOTER

Monet Dragun

www.ingramcontent.com/pod-product-compliance
Lightning Source LLC
Chambersburg PA
CBHW070519260626
47161CB00004B/1590